# Sweet Engagement

LOVE HAPPENS • BOOK FIVE

# SUSAN WARNER

# Sweet Engagement

# One

"You need to talk to Evan."

Cassandra Olsen had heard the words from her friend Skye O'Malley at the store where she worked. The words had sounded ominous, her friend was acting fidgety and no matter how she pressed, Skye wouldn't elaborate.

Evan Sparrow. She couldn't even say his name without getting flutterings in her stomach. What she needed to do was concentrate on the mechanic who was trying to tell her what was wrong with her car.

Bobby Kelly, the resident Sweet Blooms mechanic, was a decent guy. He was five foot ten, towering over Cassandra's five foot seven. Bobby looked like he'd stepped right out of the dictionary's definition of how every mechanic should look like. He was dressed in overalls stained with oil. His pockets were sagging from the tools in them, and normally he had a patient smile when he explained things to her. They had been at it for twenty minutes, and Cassandra could tell his patience was just about up.

"Okay, let's try this one more time. I'm sure I'll get it this time," Cassandra said in an upbeat, encouraging tone.

Obviously, it was the wrong tone because Bobby tensed up.

"Of course, Ms. Olsen," he said with forced patience.

"So what you're telling me is there are pistons in my engine."

"Check."

"And the reason why my car was smoking was because one of those pistons popped out. Right?"

Bobby nodded. "Ms. Olsen, it didn't just pop out. It came out through the engine block."

Cassandra nodded her head. She had heard this part of the story for the last twenty minutes. "I hear you. So what I'm saying is this: if you know what came out, get a replacement, put it back, and then patch up the block so I can get my car back."

If it was possible, Bobby turned three shades of red and told Cassandra to wait in front of the store, and he would return. Cassandra did as he asked. She knew whatever was wrong with the car was bad, but she loved this car. It was the only thing she had taken with her from her divorce.

Thinking it was taking way too long for Bobby to write up an estimate on what the problem was, she went towards the back room and saw Bobby coming towards her with a phone in hand. He handed Cassandra the phone and nodded for her to take it.

"Hello?" she asked.

"Cassandra?" asked the deep baritone on the other end. And the flutterings started before he was even on the last "a." She knew she needed to talk to him, but what was Bobby thinking to call Evan?

"Evan?" she asked. As if she didn't know who it was. "I'm not sure why Bobby called you but –"

Evan interrupted her. "He didn't call for me. He actually called for Robert. He didn't know that Robert and Delilah decided to leave early to celebrate their engagement before coming back to get married."

"Oh. Well, I'm sorry to interrupt you. I'll just let—"

"It's no interruption at all. I needed to talk to you."

Again, there were those ominous words that Cassandra had been running from. She couldn't blame this on Evan. Those were the words her ex had said to her right before he explained that the tryst he had engaged in with his personal assistant hadn't meant a thing.

"Okay, what was it?" Cassandra asked as she braced herself for the worst.

"I'll tell you when I see you."

"When you see me?"

"Yes, I'm on my way."

Cassandra was completely confused. "Why are you on the way? And why can't you just tell me now?"

"I'm coming to get you because you don't have a ride."

"I know that. That's why I'm here with Bobby, so he can fix my car!" Cassandra said, frustration seeping into her voice.

"I need you to listen to me."

Cassandra recognized that calm tone Evan was using. It was the same tone Bobby had been using on her during her stay here at the garage. She was sure that if Evan could hear what he sounded like, he would see why she was offended. Deciding to hear him out before she told him she already understood the situation, Cassandra took a deep breath and let it out.

"Go ahead, Evan."

"Bobby told me you had a piston shoot through your engine block."

Taking a deep breath and calling on all of her meditative mantras she remembered from back in the day when she did yoga, she replied, "Yes, that's what he said."

"I want to make sure you understand what that means."

"He told me the piston went through the block," she reiterated slowly.

"So you probably understand, but let me say it my way so you get the whole picture, okay?"

"Yes."

"So oil is like blood in a car."

"Got it," Cassandra said, looking at her shoes. She needed a new pair.

"The engine is like the human heart, and it pumps blood."

"Got it." After all of this, she would treat herself to a new pair while they fixed the car.

"The chambers in the heart are like pistons."

Cassandra heard what Evan said, and she stopped looking at her shoes.

"Yes," she said more slowly than before.

"The human heart is held in place by a muscle, and let's just say that's the engine block."

"Okay." Cassandra was beginning to understand what was being said, and she looked for a seat. The realization must have shown on her face because Bobby provided a chair out of nowhere and patted her shoulder.

"Now the piston going out of the engine block is like a chamber of the heart that has popped out through the muscle that surrounds the heart."

"Oh no," Cassandra moaned. "There's no way to fix my baby, is there?"

"Well, the good news is the engine isn't like the human heart. It's a lot easier to get a new engine. It's not the cheapest thing to get, and you need to decide if you want to get a new engine or buy a new car. I would tell you to get a new car."

"The baby is gone?" Cassandra moaned.

"I'm on my way." Cassandra didn't hear him hang up the phone. She didn't really notice when Bobby took the phone from her grasp either. She was too wrapped up in the fact that the last thing she had bought with her own money was gone. It was the car she had gotten when she found out she passed the CPA exam. It was a source of inspiration whenever she thought she wasn't good at anything.

Soon Evan showed up to help. It figured when she had a low moment she would be faced with him. "Thanks," she said. "You didn't really need to come —"

Evan Sparrow was just as impressive as the toys he carved. He had a beard that was always trim and tidy. Cassandra wasn't sure, but she thought the only shirts the man owned were white tee shirts and how he worked all day and always kept them clean was a mystery to her.

Since Evan had shown up, the general consensus was that Evan gave new meaning to country strong and American made. On top of his physically fit body, trimmed beard, and brown sable eyes, the air of country fresh seemed to follow him around. Plus, he had the added benefit of being a nice person.

Cassandra had been bowled over by his gentlemanly behavior when he'd invited her to an outing a couple of weeks ago. He'd held the door for her, and he never rushed her. Evan lived on the edge of town in what was called by the town's people *the swampies*. Cassandra wasn't from Sweet Blooms, but she could tell there was more to the name *swampies* than anyone wanted to explain.

When people used the expression *one of the good guys*, Cassandra was sure you'd see Evan's face there. Everyone in the town would agree Evan was patient, polite and not hard to look at either.

The corner of his mouth was lifted just enough to see his pearly white teeth. "I've come to save you."

The statement broke Cassandra out of her meanderings. "I'm glad you're doing the neighborly thing, but this is in no way saving me. I stopped believing in white knights when I was five."

Both sides of his perfect mouth turned up and became a smile. "You're welcome, princess," he said, holding out his hand. "Your carriage awaits."

Cassandra smiled at him, rolled her eyes, and then walked past him to his truck. When she looked over her shoulder, she saw what had been a smile was now a full-fledged grin. He made her remember that simple things were the best to be grateful for.

"Thank you for coming, Evan, and for explaining it to me. If you could drop me at my place, I'd appreciate it," Cassandra asked. Evan nodded, and both of them got into his truck. After Evan had turned the key and started the truck, Cassandra turned towards him and asked the question that was hanging in the air like the proverbial elephant.

"Okay, Evan, what is it that you need to talk to me about?"

Evan tightened his hands around the steering wheel. He'd worked for hours practicing what to say to Cassandra. He had tortured his friend Tom into listening to him explain what the bracelet meant and how he had thought she was on the same page.

Now they were in the car going to her place, and there was no mood. There was no ambiance, even though Tom had stated he was sure that Evan needed it. According to Tom, city women were different. Tom was a soon-to-be dad, but he had dated a city woman a time or two, and he was always confused when dealing with them.

If Evan had been able to choose the place, it surely would not have been in his truck after her favorite car had died. Evan pulled himself together and tried to think about what it was that he could say to her now.

"What do you know about the traditions in Sweet Blooms?" he asked instead.

"Umm, I've been here for more than a year. We've been out a couple of times. You've given me a gift even. I can't say we've ever discussed Sweet Blooms traditions. What has that got to do with what you wanted to talk about anyway?"

"I think I want to answer the question tomorrow, if you'll go out with me?" Evan was driving and couldn't see her response.

"When you get to Morris Street, why don't you turn there so I can see if everything is okay with my neighbor?"

Evan cleared his throat. "I'm not familiar with that road. Can you just let me know when it's coming up, and I'll turn there?"

Cassandra laughed and shook her head. "You're not familiar with that road? It's the main road through a third of the town," she said incredulously.

Evan shrugged. "I'm a recent transplant to driving through the town."

"That's right; you lived on the outskirts of town before you came to represent the guild."

Evan waited for the prejudice and bias to color her voice, but it never came. He should have known better than to expect that sort of behavior from Cassandra. One more clue that she wasn't Sweet Blooms born.

"Are you going to tell me about where you grew up?" she asked quietly.

Evan smiled. It was good that she was curious about him. Right now, he needed some signs that he hadn't imagined the attraction between them and that she wanted to be in a relationship with him. As far as he was concerned, questions were good.

"I'm going to answer any questions you want tomorrow."

"Hey, you passed Morris."

"I'm sorry. I thought you lived down this road. I was so focused on you that I missed it."

Cassandra shook her head and smiled. "How can I get upset with that? When a man says the reason he didn't do something was because a woman was too much of a distraction, he gets a pass."

Evan brought them to the front of the house. Cassandra pushed open the door and then turned back to him. "Until tomorrow then?"

"I'll come for you tomorrow, and we'll talk and go riding."

"It's a deal," Cassandra said.

"It's a date," Evan said.

# *Two*

Cassandra met Evan at Lorry stables. He had texted a picture of the stable last night but everyone in Sweet Blooms knew about the Lorry stables.

She wasn't really sure what to expect, but she was excited to see Evan. The last couple of outings they had together had been pleasant and he had been nothing short of a perfect gentleman.

She wasn't one to rush into anything but all of the signs said Evan was one of the good guys. He wasn't very vocal about his feelings but he was sincere. She knew that when he had given her a bracelet at their last date.

With the sun out, the trails were clear and Lorry stables boasted green trails and pretty flowers. Although, Cassandra was sure she wasn't going to be able to recall any of the flowers she saw today. After all, Evan had turned their meeting into a date. She'd decided to wear blue jeans and a casual wine colored top. She wanted to look natural but chic. Her hair was up in a bun, and she had let some tendrils fall strategically down the side of her face.

"Are you ready?" he asked with a wide grin.

"As ready as I'll ever be," she said.

When she'd woken up this morning, she thought about calling him and telling him she couldn't make it. Cassandra had already learned from her first marriage that relationships between people who worked with each other didn't end well. Evan was a great supplier of product to the store. He had built up a following that came in for his carvings. She didn't want to be the cause of any interruption in business because of what did or didn't happen between her and Evan. She'd had that thought all through her shower, but after she had put on her outfit and approved of the image looking back, she'd changed her mind. It was just a first time that he had called it a date. Finally, she could say they were dating. She supposed he needed to give her a gift before he thought they were dating. Odd, but Sweet Blooms is a small town. It wasn't like they were discussing children and marriage.

They both mounted their horses and started down the trail.

"We'll go to the pond and back, okay?" he asked. She'd been to this farm before, and the horses knew the way even if the people got lost. The pond was on the trail, and there was shade and a place for the horses to take a break. She nodded and off they went.

Cassandra waited for five minutes before she started taking sly looks next to her. Ten minutes in, she turned to Evan and found him smiling.

"I guess quiet contemplation wasn't high on your list as a child," Evan joked.

Cassandra agreed. "I was the one who looked at the teacher's desk as I was going by to see what the lesson was going to be that day."

"I wasn't raised in town. You'll find those of us who live on the outskirts have a different temperament and a different way when it comes to time."

"And that is?"

"It'll happen when it's time and not a second before," he answered.

Cassandra wanted to scream. He was going to drive her crazy with this zen attitude. It had only been ten minutes, and he hadn't said a thing.

*Keep it together girl,* she reminded herself.

Before she came to Sweet Blooms, she was one of the most sought after auditors and advisor to CFO's. She knew the value of patience and waiting. As the horses trotted along, her skill for remaining calm and not jumping the gun seemed to have vanished.

Thankfully, the pond came into view. With something else to focus on, she steered her horse towards the pond. When he followed, she just kept repeating to herself, *patience is a virtue.*

"You know my family has been living in what they call the 'swamp' area for the better part of four generations."

"Is there really a swamp? I mean, I look at you, Evan, and I have to say you're not what I imagine a swamp dweller looks like."

He smiled. "Well, we don't live in the swamp proper. We do have electricity and plumbing. And it's probably more accurate to say we live on the edges of the town. Our backyards face the swamp. So it wouldn't be a surprise if I woke up to a crocodile in my backyard."

"I take that to mean you don't have any pets in the backyard," she said. A shiver went through her when she recalled Florida was one of the only places that crocodiles and alligators coexisted together.

"No, I don't, but I'm thinking I want to move into town permanently and find a nice townhome to settle into."

Cassandra smiled. "I'm sure Skye will be thrilled to have you in town. It will remove the whole delay she has when you mail in your toys once a month. Now she'll be able to get them as they're made," she said excitedly.

Evan shrugged. "It may be a benefit to her. I'm moving here because I feel like it's time I started thinking about settling down."

She heard the words and her whole body tensed up. The horse jerked forward, reminding her that she was still astride and by squeezing her legs, she had urged the horse to jerk forward. "I didn't know that was something you were interested in."

Evan looked confused. "Isn't everyone interested in finding someone, so they aren't alone?"

Cassandra gave him another look. "We all may want to be with someone, but I wouldn't say you're at the age to settle down."

"I didn't realize I had to be past my prime to look at settling down," he said.

Cassandra shrugged. "I'm not saying you have to be past your prime. I'm saying that's usually when people start to think about it. When they're on the downtrend. That's all." Not liking the way the conversation was going, she dismounted. She walked her horse over to a large tree and took a seat.

"So people in the city start to look for a partner when they are on the downward trend?" Evan asked.

Cassandra glanced at Evan and then let out a big breath. "I can't speak for the whole city, but I can say most people in the city are job focused. They want to make sure they can work and make their money upfront. I think in the later years of their careers, that's when they start to think of who they'll share their lives with."

"I think you're going to find that Sweet Blooms has a rhythm of its own when it comes to settling down. It just happens," Evan said with a smile.

Evan didn't understand. She'd already been led down the *let's get settled down* road. The road scared her to no end these days. She knew it was a contradiction. She wanted a relationship, but she didn't want to think about it growing into marriage. Cassandra knew at some point she had to address this fear, but not now.

"How long have you been doing carvings?" she asked. It wasn't a smooth change in topic, but it would have to do.

"All of my life. My father taught me, and his dad taught him."

"Did they all sell their crafts?"

Evan smiled. "No, my dad would say he had no use for city money. If he needed it, then God would put it in the ground for him to find or grow."

"Your mother was born here too?"

"No, my mom worked with a real estate company in town. She'd been brought in by a realtor, or so the story goes. She was going to convince my dad to sell his land. It was a specialty of hers, acquisitions. At any rate, she came and they fell in love, and instead of getting him off of the land, she made sure he could stay on his property."

Cassandra looked at that little boy smile spread across his face.

"You're teasing me because I'm not from Sweet Blooms."

He held up his hands in defense, standing in front of his horse. "You can ask in town. Everyone knows the story."

"And they lived happily ever after?" she teased.

Evan shrugged. "I think they lived most of the time happy. They weathered a lot, stood by each other, and they loved each other."

Cassandra wouldn't touch that statement at all. Everyone always thought the couple was happy. She didn't want to argue or disillusion him, so she did what she was good at: she changed the subject. Besides she didn't know the fate of the couple and she didn't want to break the mode with her negative thoughts.

"When did you start carving for money?"

Evan looked up as if he were thinking. "I did it the summer my dad got sick. I'd been sitting by his bed after his heart attack. I had been doing some basic whittling, and then other people came looking for similar toys. With dad not working, I needed the cash, and I could still stay at home and help my mom out."

"It came just in the nick of time."

"I didn't think so. I was young, in my late teens. I thought it wasn't a real job. I tried to get some small time jobs to get employment. After a couple of months I found out that I could make the same money I was making by carving out toys. That was when I put my pride on the side and really started to carve with the intent of making money."

Cassandra smiled. "Well, Skye is very happy with your decision to move into town and to carve more product."

"It's true that one of the reasons I moved to town was to help Robert in representing the group."

"And the other?"

Evan smiled. "I'm looking to, as you say, settle down on the downtrend of my life. I think by staying in town, I can get the woman I'm looking for."

Cassandra looked into Evan's eyes, and where his smile would cause a quickening in her stomach, today it caused a tightness in her chest. "Well, good luck with that. I think we should be getting back."

Evan reached out for her hand. "I told you, this is Sweet Blooms; it has its own timing. I learned love can just happen."

Cassandra gently pulled her hand back. "Maybe it can happen with some people, but I'm not one of them." She stepped back and mounted her horse. Evan looked up at her in the saddle.

"I have to tell you something," Evan said.

The tightness was going up a notch. "Yes?"

"Did you like the bracelet I gave you?"

Cassandra was confused. "Yes, I do. See?" she said as she held out her hand so he could see the bracelet.

"It's a custom of the people who live on the edge of town. When they see a woman they like, they give her a token that she can wear for a year and a day until they decide if they'd like to be together."

Cassandra looked at her wrist and then looked at Evan. The bracelet was made of individual carved wooden spheres. On closer inspection it looked like each sphere had a carving within it. She could feel her eyebrow lift. "Are you saying that when you gave me this bracelet, it was like saying we're going out?"

Evan nodded. "I thought you knew, but I can see —"

Cassandra started to tug at the bracelet. "No!"

Evan reached out and stopped her from tugging at her wrist. "It can only be given once. Even if you don't want it, I can't take it back, and it would never go to another woman."

Fear and anger coalesced into a perfect storm.

"I am not going to change my life because of some backwoods traditions."

She could see his smile falling away, replaced by a bland expression.

"We live on the outskirts, and we have running water and electricity in our homes," he said tightly.

Cassandra just shook her head in disagreement. "No, no, no. I'm just saying I'm not going to get roped into doing something based on some archaic tradition."

"It's old, and it works. A man gives a woman a token, then they get to know each other for a year before they commit to anything long-term. Sometimes they make the year and sometimes they don't but it was always a good test run. It's called hand fasting"

Cassandra couldn't hear anything Evan said. The only thing she knew was he was trying to trap her.

"You don't have the right to trap me. I'll make sure you get your bracelet back. But I'm not like you and your kind. Maybe this works for you swampies, but it won't and can't work for me."

She didn't wait for a response; instead, she spurred the horse and went back to the barn. Never again would she settle down and be a good wife. She wasn't going to fall for the same trick twice.

Cassandra was in the store at five the next morning. It was earlier than expected but nearly as early as she needed to be. Yesterday's conversation had stayed with her all day and all night. Normally, when she did come in early, it was to look at the new toys from Evan. Today, looking at the items on the shelf dedicated to him brought her no peace.

When the store opened, she hoped to lose herself in the clients. Sweet Blooms was at the end of its festival days, so there were still some tourists left. Today, the only thing they all wanted to look at was Evan's shelf. They asked questions, wondering if she knew the artist and if she knew where he got his inspiration. She remembered to smile and shake her head vacantly while offering them a good price.

After a sale, she'd get a boost, but the regular things she did to make herself happy weren't working. She knew why they weren't working and that reason had a name: Evan Sparrow.

She'd had enough time to know she had overreacted. She didn't realize how sensitive she was about the issue, but by the time she'd had time to think it through, she was home in bed and Evan was long gone from the farm.

She'd tossed her reaction around, trying to understand what had occurred. Cassandra was disappointed in herself. She thought she had gotten over the foolishness of her ex. It appeared her brain thought they had gotten over the betrayal, but when it came down to it, she had lashed out at a person who hadn't earned it.

She knew the situation she found herself in now was her fault. She had taken the bracelet. She had the bracelet on now in fact. She looked down at the circle around her wrist and fingered the clasp.

She was going to fix this. She just needed to get enough courage to face Evan.

When Skye came in today for work, she would go see Evan at his place or call him and find out if he was in the woodcarver's house at the Cade place.

All of those plans went south when the front bell tinkled and Evan Sparrow walked into the store with his box of toys. He wasn't loud or rude; in fact, it might have been because he didn't make a big fuss either way that everyone noticed him. He didn't slam the door when he walked in; instead, he made sure to hold it until it closed silently. To do that, he had to do a 180 degree twist at the waist that had more than one eye looking at his lean body.

Cassandra was transfixed watching him walk into the store carrying the box. He was completely clothed, yet the subtle pulls across the muscles of his arms showed through his t-shirt.

He had on his standard gear: blue jeans and a white t-shirt. It wasn't the clothing that made him stand out, it was just Evan. Cassandra could make the case that he was an attractive package, but she knew it was more.

When he looked up and saw her at the counter, he paused. She felt lower than the bottom of a snake's belly. She had been wrong to judge him, even in anger, yesterday. She had been so blinded by her past that she couldn't see him, she'd lashed out at him when it was another man altogether who had caused her heartache.

When he saw she wasn't moving, he came to the counter and placed the box down. He kept her gaze and didn't smile as he waited.

She couldn't let this go. "I need to talk to you about yesterday."

Serious eyes tracked her, giving nothing away. His gaze didn't soften. She wasn't greeted by the infectious smile that made any troubles she had fade away.

"You could at least meet me halfway here," she said as she stood as tall as she could. "I was wrong to judge you like I did yesterday. I know it didn't make sense to you, but I was reliving something in my past that I thought I had gotten over, but obviously, I haven't."

He pushed the box to the side and then leaned his hip against the counter. "I have to tell you, as far as apologies go, that one was pretty bad."

Cassandra's mouth fell open and then she looked back at Evan. "I gave that apology all on my own. I didn't have a conference or a meeting."

Evan nodded. "Yes, I can tell you made that one up all by yourself, the delivery and all."

"Kick rocks!" she grumbled, then went to the box and gingerly opened it. As she took the toys out, she gave each item more praise than the last. "The community center is going to love when you start teaching there. I'm not sure if people will be coming to see you work or to get a toy made by you."

"They'll be waiting a while. I won't start any classes until we get to the last class in the lesson plan worked out."

"Really? Have you told Ms. Waters?"

"Nope, I think I'll run it past the board first."

Cassandra wanted to warn him that Sandra Waters liked to approve the things that went on in the community center before the board heard it. Her friend Hannah worked there, and she told Cassandra and Skye stories of how Sandra Waters was a woman unto herself. "I think if you have an idea, you should make sure you're comfortable with it first. As long as you have a plan, then it should all be well."

"Do you want to review my plan to make sure I've included everything?"

"No. I'm not going to stick my nose into things I don't know anything about."

"No matter how backward I may be?"

Cassandra shook her head and gave him an aggravated look. "I said I was sorry. Be happy with it."

"Seriously, I do want you to take a look at my numbers."

"Why me?"

"I want a fresh perspective to look at my numbers. I know Robert, Adam, and Hannah have looked at them, but they all have a vision when they see the plan, so I don't think they are the most objective people I could have found."

Cassandra paused and then nodded. It figured; even after she had acted too out of character, he was willing to trust her with his business. She found him to be very accepting so she nodded in agreeance.

"No problem. I'll do it."

"Thanks," Evan said with a smile.

That man had a smile that made Cassandra give him a second look. His smile gave her flutterings in her stomach, and made her smile widely in response. When Evan said he'd see her later, she just nodded.

After the door had closed and he was out of the store, she had enough time to think about her reaction to Evan. She had to come to grips with what he had told her about the bracelet, and not just dismiss it as a fluke.

When a customer came up to her and asked about finding a gift, she pulled herself together and focused on the task at hand.

She wasn't ready to buy into the whole handfasting thing, but she was willing to say she liked Evan, obviously. Evan wasn't her ex, Michael. Evan hadn't lied to her, nor had he cheated on her. The next time they spoke, she was going to have to broach the subject of their handfasting.

The day was going pretty good for Evan. After leaving Cassandra, he realized things were getting back on track. They hadn't discussed the bracelet, but they were talking. Now all he had to do was get through the community meeting. Robert had already met with the board, but now that Evan had made some changes, they wanted to review what had been agreed upon. Evan thought they should call Robert back, but when Robert asked him to go talk for himself, he agreed.

He had been a little anxious meeting with the board for other reasons. Now that he was talking to Cassandra and had given her the bracelet, his intentions were clear. He needed to make sure the community center would honor their part. There'd be no sense in having a partner but not having a way to take care of her.

Robert told him Sandra Waters wasn't happy with the woodworking site the Cades had built on their farm. Part of her not protesting the shop and tying it up in a legal battle was on the promise that Evan would teach classes at the community center. She wanted to make sure everyone had an equal chance and more than anyone Evan inspired those feelings in her. Still, Evan wanted to be prepared if they asked any questions so he could talk to them without having to read a long document in the board meeting.

He walked into the room, and there was Clarissa, Mayor Mason, and Sandra Waters. He looked around the room and realized that no one else was there. They had set up a table in front of the women, and Evan felt more like he was going to a questioning rather than a negotiation.

He thought about Cassandra and took a seat. What he did today in this room would have a long term effect on what kind of future he could have in town. Evan thought about how Cassandra had faced her fear by apologizing. She was a beautiful woman on the outside, and on the inside where it mattered. She didn't let her pride get in the way and apologized to him even though he knew it couldn't have been easy. He was going to face his fear as well.

Mayor Mason gestured for him to take a seat. "Hello Evan Sparrow, we're all here to make sure we have all of the details worked out regarding the relationship between you and the community center, which is owned by Sandra Waters."

The mayor picked up the paper in front of her and then looked at Evan. "I'm sorry, did you want a recap of the details as well?"

Evan saw the paper and flinched. This would all go south if someone asked him to read it. He shook his head and looked at Clarissa, who gave him a slight nod.

"Ms. Mayor, I think we should be able to talk about

this. Afterward, you can write it up, but I'm from the outskirts of town. We do a lot of our business based on a person's word. I understand that's not how it's done in town. I am willing to let you all write up whatever we decide, but I'd like to talk it through first."

The Mayor looked at both ends of the table, and both women nodded in agreement.

"Okay, Evan, let's go review what we have. Ms. Waters will start."

Sandra Waters was in her fifties, with black hair. Evan thought she was taller than most women in Sweet Blooms at probably around five foot ten.

"Thank you, Mr. Sparrow, for coming out."

Evan interrupted her. "Ms. Waters, we're about to do business. You can call me Evan."

Ms. Waters looked at the Mayor, who gave her a smile and nodded.

"Well, Evan, the Cades have built a woodworking shop on their property. While we are all very happy Adam Cade has come back home and brought the publicity of a hometown millionaire living here, it leaves me in a precarious position."

"I see how that could interrupt some of your business, but Cade's design is for woodworkers. It's not really for the hobbyist. We'll give a seminar and even sell some items, but the woodworking shop is primarily for professionals to have some place to work."

Ms. Waters pursed her lips during his explanation and then nodded. "I'm sure that the intention right now is for him to be open for professionals, but Mr. Cade is a businessman and a successful one. I have to protect my livelihood as well. When and if Mr. Cade realizes there's money to be made by giving classes to everyone, my center will essentially be put out of business. Sweet Blooms Community Center is the hub for crafts to be taught. We are going under renovation and have several people coming to help us expand. All of that planning will be for nothing if Cade Designs decides to open their teaching doors."

Evan looked at the woman and heard the anxious tones coming from Ms. Waters. "I understand your point of view. I'm willing to help, but I want to make sure we understand my end. I make toys and carvings for the general store. Robert Parker started the guild, and I'm one of the leaders. To make sure the center stays open, I'll teach a couple of classes there. I'd like some things in return."

Evan looked at Clarissa who sat back in her chair and smiled. She folded her arms under her chest and rocked. Mayor Mason looked to Ms. Waters, and Evan could see Ms. Waters was already sputtering.

"We've been very generous with you, Mr. Sparrow. The town has agreed to buy you a house."

"And you've got the first choice on classes in your center. I'm willing to do that, but only for three classes a week," Evan replied.

Ms. Waters shook her head. "I won't be dictated to about how many classes I can have in my business." She turned towards the mayor and started complaining. "You see, it's already started."

Mayor Mason held up her hand to stop Ms. Waters and then turned to Evan.

"Is there a reason for this, Evan? When Mr. Parker came, he gave us assurances that you would cooperate. It seems like now that the woodworking center is done, things are changing."

He saw the shrewd look in her eyes and knew no matter how loud Ms. Waters was, the mayor was the one in control.

"I'm not changing things, Ms. Mayor. I just need time to work on items for myself. I have a contract with the general store, and I'm going to be helping the professsionals at the woodworking shop. I don't mind classes but I need to make sure I have enough to live on."

Ms. Waters interrupted. "You ought to. We're giving you a house."

Evan ignored Ms. Waters and looked the mayor in the eye. "The house was my request. I'm leaving the outskirts so I can be close enough if Ms. Waters needs me and to get to the classes on time. I also have to think about possibly having a family in town."

For the first time, Clarissa spoke. "And is that your intention, Evan? To settle down within the town limits of Sweet Blooms?"

Before Evan could answer, Ms. Waters did. "Please, Clarissa, we don't need to know the availability of every man in Sweet Blooms, do we?"

Evan let the question go and looked back at the mayor. The mayor leaned back before speaking. "What else do you want, Evan?"

"More?" said Ms. Waters incredulously. "I can't believe we are dealing with a swampie and offering him everything when it's my life that is being disrupted. I have a son to take care of, and that seems like it's being put to the side."

Evan let the swampie comment go by him. He realized that it was going to come up sooner or later. He hadn't let it stop him from doing anything else, and he wasn't going to let it get in his way now. Although, if he were honest with himself, he'd say that he wondered if that was a concern for Cassandra. Would she swayed by petty people who might judge her for hanging out with the wrong element? He knew she was a strong woman, but small towns could be the best and the worst places. When you're part of the town, everyone is with you, but when they all decide you're on the outside, they could kill you with kindness.

"Ms. Waters, I'm not here to make your life difficult. I'm about to give up the life I know. I want to make sure I can support myself and be a productive part of the town."

The mayor cleared her throat. "Evan, while I disagree with Ms. Waters' choice of words, I have to say that I wanted to ask you if you were okay relocating. I realize it was a part of the plan, but if you don't want to move to town, I don't want you to feel forced."

He could see Ms. Waters looking incredulously at the mayor. He wasn't sure if he should be happy she was offering him a choice or upset that she thought he could be bullied or pushed into making this move even though he didn't want to.

"I'm ready for a change," Evan said.

"You know if you stayed in your home and donated your time, it would be a benefit to the town."

Clarissa looked down the table at Ms. Waters. "Really, Sandra? You talk about me, but you'd take advantage of him just because of where he lives?"

"Enough." Mayor Mason said, her tone brooking no discussion. She looked to Evan. "Clarissa provided your requests to us. Let us get back to you on the new items, but I don't foresee a problem. Thank you for coming today. We appreciate your openness to discuss this delicate matter."

Evan nodded to the women as he walked out the door. Clarissa winked at him, and he smiled.

# Three

Evan walked out of the room and waited in front of City Hall. He was happy to get out of the building. He thought the reference to him being a swampie wouldn't bother him, but on some level, it just frustrated him. He had grown up with the title, but he knew it wasn't so easy for his parents. His dad was from the outskirts, but his mom went through an adjustment period. He wondered if Cassandra would have to go through that as well. She wasn't from Sweet Blooms and making the change to a small town could be stressful for some women. He wasn't living on the outskirts, but he knew for some people they would only know him as a swampie.

"Well, I can't change it by worrying about it," he muttered under his breath.

"Ain't that the truth," replied Clarissa from over his shoulder. She was standing on a step one higher than him, so they were eye to eye. He didn't understand Clarissa. She wore tight clothing to accentuate a curvaceous body, and he knew her reputation. He didn't understand why she let them think the worst.

Clarissa handed him some papers. "They say the

same thing we went over before. There was nothing new added. It's been filed in the board minutes, and you should receive a copy like this with a seal on it in about seven days."

Evan took the paper and nodded to Clarissa. "Thanks."

She smiled at him, and he knew she was about to be devilish. "If you're feeling so thankful, you could answer my question."

"Your question?" Evan said, hoping it wasn't what he thought it was.

"Yes, Evan Sparrow. Have you decided to settle down with a townie?"

He took a step back and smiled back before he replied. "Clarissa, it's not about if I've decided to settle down with a woman, it's if she's decided she wants me."

With that, he nodded and walked away. With all the talking about the woman he wanted to settle down with, he decided it was time to visit that very woman for lunch.

He went to the store hoping to find Cassandra operating the cash register so he could suggest lunch. Instead, he found Skye operating the register and Cassandra with Ms. Waters. Evan was hoping to slip into the store and wait in the back until Ms. Waters had left. He thought the crowd was enough to hide him as he made his way through the store. However, luck was not on his side.

"Mr. Sparrow," Ms. Waters said, waving her hand in the air as if he couldn't hear her. Her need to call him Mr. Sparrow grated on his nerves.

"Evan," Cassandra said. She looked a little tense, so Evan smiled a little more and focused on Ms. Waters.

"I can see you found the best shop in town to go browsing in," Evan said.

Ms. Waters grunted. "I came in here to see what kind of work I would be getting when you started classes. I think when you do classes and products for the center, they should be unique to the center."

Evan smiled and just as casually replied with, "I don't believe there is anything in the papers or in the conversation today about me making product for the center, or me making unique items."

Ms. Waters' expression became tight, and she looked at the shelves and then back at Evan. "Perhaps that was an oversight on my part. Certainly, looking at the inventory here and considering the work that will be done on the Cade site, it should be a consideration that the community center has its own unique items. I'm saying that to remain competitive, it should be a consideration."

Cassandra watched as Sandra talked to Evan, and she could see him tensing up the longer Sandra kept talking. Evan clearly wasn't comfortable, but she didn't know how to interrupt the conversation. What made it worse was she felt that this conversation was a continuation of something else.

She knew Evan had already made a lot of concessions by moving to town. The other requests Sandra was asking from him were beyond what was needed. Listening to the way Sandra was trying to get him to agree to this new proposal, she had to wonder what made Evan do this at all.

The silence between the two had stretched a couple of seconds past comfortable, and Cassandra wanted to end it before something was said that would cause more tension between the two.

"I hate to be the one to interrupt, but Evan is here to take me to lunch," Cassandra said.

Sandra looked at them both and then nodded. "Well, I won't keep you, but Mr. Sparrow, do think on my proposal." After nodding to both parties, she walked out the door.

"Ironically, I did come to take you to lunch. After that rescue, you can pick where you would like to eat," he said with a smile.

That smile. It made her forget what she was thinking about. When she saw it, she got all giddy and just wanted to stare at him. Shaking herself internally, Cassandra pulled herself together. She wasn't a teenager mooning over a man.

"Let's go to Banter House. If we hurry, we can get there before the lunch crowd."

Evan nodded, and they went to Banter House down the way. Cassandra was thrilled to hear he had come to take her to lunch. She wasn't sure if she had turned him away, and she wanted to talk to him about the bracelet and them.

When they arrived at Banter House, she stood at the hostess pulpit. When Evan kept walking, she grabbed him by the arm. He looked at her confused. Cassandra pointed to the sign.

"Evan, it says to wait to be seated."

Evan looked at the sign and shrugged. "Geeta lets me seat myself."

Cassandra paused and then gestured for him to lead the way. Evan went to a booth that seemed like it was second nature to him.

They must have been sitting for ten minutes before Cassandra noticed their waitress hadn't come over. No one had even come to the table to offer water. Evan had his menu face down, and he seemed as though he was waiting. Cassandra looked around the restaurant and saw two of the waitresses looking but not trying to get caught looking at Evan.

"You make quite an impression on the staff," she said.

Evan smiled a half smile. "The impression is probably not what you think."

Confused, Cassandra looked again, and the girls had disappeared. Coming towards them was the round Indian owner, Geeta. She looked frustrated. Her hair was wrapped up in a bun on her head, and she had a small notepad.

One of the other waitresses was coming up behind Evan, and Cassandra heard a word or two of their whisperings. The words "look" and "a real swampie" floated in the air. Evan didn't turn around; instead, he kept his gaze on Cassandra.

Geeta finally got to the table.

"Evan, it's been too long. All of the girls are wondering if the end of the world is coming with you being here. What do you want to eat?"

Evan nodded towards Cassandra. After all of the orders were taken, Geeta leaned down and hugged Evan.

"It's been too long since you let me feed you."

"I'm moving to town so you'll be feeding me more often."

Geeta looked between him and Cassandra. "Well, I hope it all works out for you."

When Geeta left, Cassandra decided she was tired of the cloak and dagger code that was going on.

"Okay, what's going on? Why are people acting weird?" Cassandra asked.

"I thought when I cleaned up and became the head of the guild I would be treated a little differently," he said as he looked around the floor.

Cassandra was confused. "What are you talking about?"

Evan smiled. "I keep forgetting you've only been here, what, about two years?"

"Yeah, just about."

"So I'm sure you know by now that I live on the outskirts of town."

Cassandra smiled. "I remember when you took me to the campfire party out by your place, or was I not supposed to notice that we drove by every house in town?"

He shrugged. "I guess that was a clue."

She saw him try to act dismissive about it, but she could see he was getting tense again.

"Evan, what is it?"

"I want you to know that no matter where I go in this town, there will always be people who remember that I lived on the outskirts where the swampies live."

She held up her hands in defense. "I've heard this term, but I ignore it."

Evan looked at her in the eye. "Can you?"

Cassandra still wasn't getting it. "Does this have something to do with Sandra Waters in the store?"

"In some ways, yes."

"I know you weren't happy when she brought up the idea of you making her exclusive content," she began.

"It's true, I'm not happy with it, and I'm not going to do it. I went to the board today. It was just to iron out what was already agreed on, and to add maybe one or two more points to the contract."

"If you already discussed it at the board, why was she trying to add something in the store?"

"Because I'm a swampie. Because Waters thinks she can get something extra out of me."

Cassandra winced. "I'm sorry."

"For?"

"Evan, every time I see you, you look happy and content. If someone had told me you had problems, I'd have had to say 'I know he has them because everyone has problems,' but in general, would not have said you had anything but a great life."

"Appearances can be tricky. I learned early not to let things I can't change bother me."

Cassandra raised her eyebrows. "But something is bothering you now?"

"I'm interested in you, Cassandra. I made a mistake with you though."

Cassandra knew eventually he would bring up the bracelet. She didn't realize until he said it how much it would hurt for him to want it back or, as he said, to admit that giving her the bracelet was a mistake. Without thinking about it, she began to remove the bracelet, but he placed his hand over hers to stop her.

Cassandra looked up, confused.

Evan smiled. "The mistake wasn't in giving you the bracelet. The mistake was in not telling you what the bracelet meant."

Relief. That was the only way she could describe what she felt. He was upset he hadn't explained the significance of the bracelet. Just as she was going to speak, the food came. They ate the burgers and sipped their drinks. While she ate, Cassandra had some time to think about what she wanted to say to Evan. When the plates had been taken away, she had a game plan.

"Evan, despite the way I initially acted, I want you to know I'm glad you gave me the bracelet. I think I would have liked to know the significance of it, but I do like you. I'm intrigued by your work, and I find you to be an interesting man. And I have to say it's been a minute since I've been able to see any male as a man I would be interested in."

Evan reached for her hands and covered hers with his. "Are you sure you don't want to wait a day or two and hear what the town is going to say about me? I want you to be prepared to be a hot topic until the next thing comes by the town."

Cassandra tightened her hands on his. "I'm not one to be moved by the antics of those in town, so don't worry about it. I'm not ashamed to be seen with you, Evan. It's not about what they think about you. It's about what we think that matters."

He stopped and stared at her for a moment.

Cassandra wiped her face. "What, is there food on my face?"

"No, you remind me of my mother."

Cassandra smiled. "I'm hoping that's a good thing?"

Evan smiled. "Yeah, it's the best of things."

Cassandra was getting that feeling of warmth that spread all through her body. "Do you want to tell me about her?"

"My mom was the best. I guess everyone says that," he began.

"Was she from Sweet Blooms?"

"No, but my dad was. My mom was a social butterfly. She always knew she wanted to be a mother and wife. She thought they were two of the most honored occupations a woman could have."

"But you said she was a social butterfly," Cassandra said.

"She didn't see a contradiction. She was born in the next town over so she was new to Sweet Blooms. When she came here, she wasn't prepared for the way swampies were ostracized. She went about changing that by getting the women together twice a week. She said it was to have girl talk because everyone woman needed to have girl talk every now and again."

Cassandra found herself smiling as he retold the stories.

"She was smart, funny, and a great listener," he said. "She always told me that my dad and I were a gift to her and she was grateful every day."

"I can't say I had the same lifestyle. I know my parents love me, but they also had expectations for me. Both of them are CPAs. When I left, my dad said it wasn't a problem to take a sabbatical and then come back."

Evan was confused. "You came to Sweet Blooms on sabbatical to work in the general store?"

Cassandra laughed. "No, that's not why I came. I came because my ex-husband, and ex-business partner, was a cheat, and he had stopped knowing I existed a long time ago."

"I'm sorry."

Cassandra nodded. "Don't be sorry. I think he was a great lesson that I really needed to learn."

"And the lesson was?"

"Love and trust don't go hand in hand. Just because I love you doesn't mean you can be trusted to watch my money."

"My mom watched the money."

"Seriously?"

"Yes, my dad's point of view was if he made it then she could cook it, save it, or plan with it."

When one of the waitresses came by and put down the check, they both reached for it.

"I've got this," she said.

Evan shook his head. "Not that I'm into gossip, but if you pay for this meal it will be out like wildfire that I'm homeless, and you are supplementing my income with some extra activities."

Cassandra gave in, and Geeta came to collect the check. She looked at the bottom signature and then she gave Evan a long look.

"You did good, boy. I'm sure your parents are really proud." Geeta grinned and then patted him on the shoulder.

"I've got to get to work," Cassandra said.

"That's fine. Thank you for coming," he said. As they were walking out to the door, he asked, "May I have your phone number?"

Cassandra looked at him and then nodded yes. After she had told him her number, he walked her back to the store. Cassandra turned around and looked at Evan. She took a step closer, thinking he was going to give her a kiss. Instead, Evan gave her a big hug and then whispered, "Thank you for being you."

He didn't wait for a reply; he just walked away.

Cassandra never thought the day would come when she would be wondering if a guy liked her or not. If this was the beginning of their relationship, she was in for a bumpy ride.

*Four*

Cassandra went back to the store, and Skye was waiting for her.

"I thought we were friends?"

Cassandra looked at Skye, and she held out her arms. "We are friends. What's wrong?"

"Then tell me why I have to hear that my friend is seeing Evan Sparrow. When I looked up from the register, I find that I'm all alone and a customer is kind enough to tell me that my friend has left the building with Evan Sparrow. Not only that, the other lady standing right next to her says that Evan Sparrow is going to be living in town because he wants to put down some roots with my friend Cassandra," Skye asked as she wiggled her eyebrows.

Cassandra let out a sigh of relief when she realized Skye was kidding.

"I'm not talking to you," Cassandra joked.

"You don't want me to have to go on their information do you? You know if they don't know something, it's okay that they make it up. Now come to your best friend and tell me the dirt on if you and Evan are going to date."

"No. Maybe. Yes," Cassandra said, heaving a big sigh. "We just finished having lunch and going over if I could make it being in a relationship with him."

At this time, Skye was leaning against the counter top. "Well, no matter the answer, in the last two years men have come by to date and you've said no to them all."

"I haven't said no to them all!"

Skye nodded her head and smiled at Cassandra. "I'm afraid so, sleeping beauty. You haven't even given them the time of day. So I have to ask the question. Do you like Evan Sparrow?"

Internally, Cassandra wanted to jump up and down and say, "Yes!" She looked at Skye.

"He's a nice guy. He's very upfront, and I have to tell you he almost seems too good to be true."

Skye laughed at Cassandra. "I see you forgot to say that he's also considered to be a hot catch. You need to be okay saying you're attracted to the man."

Cassandra groaned. "I don't have a lot of luck when it comes to attractive men."

Skye didn't say a thing. She just leaned against the counter with her arms folded across her chest. "It's been two years."

"Okay, I'll admit it. He's smart, attractive, and so patient that I do find Evan to be…attractive."

Skye clapped her hands. "Woo hoo! I think we are on the road to recovery."

Cassandra and Skye laughed and started to clean up the store together.

"I'm nervous, Skye," Cassandra confessed.

"Then you're on the right road."

"I think you're completely lost in the concept of love now that you and Caleb are planning on marriage."

Skye stopped and looked at the ring on her hand. "I'll admit that I'm happy and I want you to be happy too. But I also want you to know that I'm your family in town if you need it. If he doesn't do the right thing by you, just let me know, and Caleb will hunt him down."

Cassandra didn't know whether to laugh or moan. "Thank you, Skye. I hope this works out. Me dating Evan is a big move for me. He seems very genuine."

Skye moved closer to Cassandra and patted her on the shoulder to get her attention. "You only get one life. The one thing I learned from my twin's death is you should live life boldly."

Skye and Cassandra opened the store and Cassandra kept Skye's words on her mind. By the end of the day, Cassandra had made a decision. She was going to give it a go with Evan. She was going to give happiness a shot.

"I thought there would be more machinery in here," Cassandra said as she looked around the classroom Evan would be working in.

"I wasn't taught with all those machines until much later. My dad taught me how to draw first, choose wood next, and then carve. I think the people coming to the class may not be expecting that process, but it's mine," Evan said.

Cassandra stared at him for a moment before she asked, "I can see you love what you do. Are you sure you want to do it here in this classroom? There's still time to negotiate."

He nodded slowly. "Thank you for being concerned.

I'm used to working for what I want, and this is all part of the plan."

"The plan, you say? I don't think I've heard this plan."

Evan looked at Cassandra and took a deep breath. He could have told her there was no going back because he had already moved everything out of the house. All of the possessions he wanted to keep were in storage in town.

He was thirty-five years old, and he could freely admit that Cassandra was a woman who made him think of today, and tomorrow.

Women had come to Sweet Blooms. Some of them had seen him and were attracted to him because he was a swampie. Some of them were from the city, and when he brought in his carvings, they had some weird idea that being with him would be the dream of a lifetime. Evan had paid none of them any mind.

His mother had told him he'd know when the right woman came along. Looking at Cassandra as she walked through the classroom, he understood what she was talking about. When he saw the flash of his bracelet on her wrist playing peekaboo with her sleeve, it gave him hope that this wasn't just on his side.

"Hey, I want you to know that I support you and I'm here for you. I know how important it is to know you are not alone. Especially when you're doing something that's near and dear to your heart," he said.

"Thank you."

Cassandra held out her hand. The bracelet had fallen exactly right on her wrist. He took her hand and knew his mother was right. When it happens, there's no rhyme or reason. It just happens and you know they're the one.

Still, the words that he told Clarissa came back to him. He knew what he wanted, but it was all about if Cassandra wanted the same thing.

"Thank you so much for coming," Hannah Jenkins said as she ran towards the door. "If my head wasn't attached to me, sometimes I swear I'd lose that too."

Cassandra laughed. "Please, this is no imposition at all."

"You're really sure? I mean, if you're not, don't tell me now because I can't really fix it." Hannah took a deep breath and let it out. "Peaches adores you, and she's been a bit grumpy lately."

"Go, I've got Peaches." At the mention of her name, the dog in question raised her old head lazily from the couch and then let it fall again with a huff.

"Her food is in the refrigerator labeled and —"

Cassandra started to herd Hannah, who was rambling on and on about the situation, towards the door. "If I didn't need to meet up with the designer tonight, my dress wouldn't be ready, and the bridesmaids dresses wouldn't be ready and —"

Cassandra smiled. "It's no imposition, and you're making me crazy listening to that list. It sounds like reason 300 not to get married. The planning is a beast."

Hannah smiled. "You say that now, but wait until you meet the one. Then all of this crazy I'm going through will be worth it just to see him smile and have all of our friends and family witness how happy we are."

Cassandra hugged Hannah and watched her get into her car.

Cassandra had been leaving the store at the end of the day when she'd gotten a call from Hannah. Her designer had decided that she needed to get the measurements again because of a mix-up, but Hannah was watching Peaches. She didn't want to invite the designer to Delilah's house with Peaches since Peaches wasn't feeling very well. It was always good to take notice when a senior dog wasn't feeling well instead of just missing her owner.

She went into the living room, and sure enough, the tan and white pit bull lifted her head again. When Cassandra sat next to her, Peaches just rolled over to expose her belly.

"I see someone wants some belly rubs. How are you, old girl?"

Delilah had rescued Peaches from a shelter. Cassandra didn't know what her early days had been like, but Delilah was making sure her latter days were the stuff other dogs would brag about.

When it looked as though Peaches had fallen asleep, Cassandra got up and went to look at the bookcase that held pictures and mementos on it. She remembered when she had once thought she wanted a family. She had been with Michael, and she thought the world was theirs to take. When they had divorced, it had been hard on her as a woman, thinking she hadn't done something and had pushed him into another woman's arms. Later on, she realized that when Michael cheated, it was about him, not about her. It didn't hurt any less, but at least she wasn't going around toting guilt with her as well.

She thought the urge was gone until she met Evan. *You can't have a family if you don't have a partner.* Well, that wasn't true. She had been in the city long enough to know you could have a child and no partner, but that just wasn't for her.

Leaving all she knew and coming to Sweet Blooms had been a life changer for her that she didn't realize she needed. Her parents thought Sweet Blooms was too small and was filled with mean and narrow-minded people. Cassandra laughed at that statement. When she told her parents those people were everywhere, they were so offended. It was as if they believed that because a person had money or lived in the city, it automatically made it impossible to be any of those things.

Cassandra was pulled out of her reveries when she heard the doorbell. She turned, going to the door, and then she heard the keys. Peaches picked her head up and barked. The keys jangled once more, and then the door opened. Evan walked into the house, saw her, and smiled. Peaches turned her head away and just pulled her tail in tighter and went back to sleep.

"Hi, Cassandra," he said as he closed the door and brought in a shopping bag.

"Delilah isn't here."

"I know. I just left Robert's place and had to drop off their food. I'm here today playing the head cook for Peaches. I made her some food, and I told Delilah I would bring it by so Hannah could feed Peaches some food she was used to."

Cassandra started laughing as she looked at the bag. "You must have been cooking all night."

Evan shook his head. "How do you say no to Delilah? Then when she said it was for Peaches, I definitely couldn't say no."

"That explains Delilah. How did you get roped in doing it for Robert?"

Evan looked away. "I was already doing it for his hounds. It's the one thing I never had, so I spoil Robert's dogs when I see them."

"So, master chef, tell me what you've brought, and we can go put it in the kitchen. I take it since the queen has not risen from the couch that she's not hungry now."

Cassandra listened as Evan went on about preparing the food. She liked how he threw himself in to whatever he was doing. He wasn't worried about what people thought or how it was perceived because he was comfortable with himself and confident in what he did.

Cassandra thought about how image mattered to her when she had been married to Michael. In fact, fear of what others would say played a part in her staying with him. Moving to Sweet Blooms had been a type of therapy. She'd like to think she had outgrown the need for others' approval and that she had more freedom to live the way she wanted to without checking with everyone.

Still, when she looked at Evan, she saw a man who was more courageous than her. He walked into places with his head held high, knowing they were judging him, and in some cases finding him less no matter what he said. The slights weren't always brazen, but she could see how people could unknowingly start to whittle at him. Evan didn't get upset; he didn't acknowledge it or defend himself. That was a different kind of strength and character that she admired but didn't know if she would ever be able to have.

It was ironic to Cassandra that once again she might have the opportunity to have her dream of a family and a partner. This time it wasn't that she was being judged if she failed to stay in a relationship. This time she would be judged if she even started a relationship with Evan.

She needed to make a decision and stick to it. Since she had decided not to be alone, there was only one way to go: forward.

*Five*

Evan had waited a couple of days after seeing her at Delilah's house. He had been creating some new carvings, and he thought it was wise to give her some time to think about what he had said. He'd left her a note asking if he could come by her house and talk to her, and she had agreed.

Evan knew which condo she had rented. She was basically around the corner from Delilah. Her block was distinctive because there was a huge sign with hydrangeas on it. It was called the hydrangea block. When he arrived, the first floor looked empty. When he rang the doorbell, he heard her voice on the intercom.

"Come on up."

He opened the door and was in a narrow hall that led to a flight of steps that ended with a blue door. Just as he had finished climbing the steps, the door opened.

"I'm glad you're here. Come in."

She stepped back and gestured for him to enter. As he passed by, he could tell she was a bit out of breath.

"I'm sorry, did I come at a bad time?" he asked.

"No, no, I was just doing some last minute clean ups."

Evan nodded and continued into her coop. It was full of blues and yellows on the walls. The floor was covered in throw rugs, and there was only one couch in the living room. The windows had blinds on them, and on the other wall, there was a television mounted.

"Take a seat."

He sat on one side of the couch, and she sat down on the other. The couch was a floral print with oversized cushions. There were some little throw pillows that had sayings like *I am what I am* and *Knowing is half the battle*. He picked up one of them and looked at Cassandra. She had a flush to her face when he showed her.

She reached out and grabbed the pillow. "You didn't come here to talk about my excellent taste in cartoon viewing." He could see she was nervous and decided he needed to put her at ease as soon as possible.

He realized he was about to take a big risk and he wanted to rest in the calm before the potential storm. Cassandra was dressed in baggy sweats and a t-shirt. Her hair was up in a knot, and she was sitting cross-legged across from him. He could see she had tried to contain her hair, but strands still escaped, causing wisps to fly about her temples.

"I wanted to give you a clear picture of where we are and what I'm asking you tonight. I want you to know I don't expect an answer, but I want you to start thinking about it," Evan said.

"Okay, what is it?"

"I want you to understand what's being offered."

"Being offered?" Cassandra asked.

"Yes, you need to know what's on the table, so let's start there. First, I've never been out of Sweet Blooms. I watch lots of television. I'm not concerned about money as long as I can take care of me and my own. I can carve. I can carve and draw just about anything that I see or imagine. I don't want to go to a city or be in a museum with my work."

Cassandra looked a little confused. "I'm glad you know those things about yourself."

"Once upon a time, a woman came; her name was Brenda. She came here because she had seen my work. She thought that if she offered me enough money and pretended to be in love with me that I would leave all that I knew and follow her. It didn't work."

Cassandra reached out her hand and placed it on top of his knee. "Did you care for her?"

Evan stopped and placed his hand over hers, then smiled. "Did I tell you? You are amazing."

Cassandra gave a crooked smile. "Really?"

"You are the second person who has ever asked me that. Everyone else knew what was going on, but no one ever asked me if I had any feelings for her."

"Ouch!"

"Moving along, needless to say, she left. She made a big spectacle of it. She went through the town saying there was something wrong with me. She claimed she knew there was something wrong with me because I wouldn't have sex with her."

Cassandra nodded and waited. "Okay?"

Evan laughed. "I can see you need some more help with the last part."

"That you didn't sleep with her?"

Evan nodded. "Yes."

"No, I don't need any help with that. If you don't feel the attraction to another person, then you just don't."

Evan picked up their hands and brought hers to his lips. He placed a slow kiss on her hands.

"The point is, I've never wanted to sleep with any woman, until now. I think I may have found the right one to be with."

He watched Cassandra look at him for a moment and then he saw when what he was saying began to dawn on her.

"Oh! You mean you've never?"

Evan laughed at her shocked expression. "That's right. I never met the one. I never cared, and I was never in a rush. I want you to know because it might matter to you.

"The other thing is, I want to stay in Sweet Blooms. I know there are lots of opportunities for what I do in the city. In fact, every five months or so a recruiter comes down in the hopes of changing my mind about going to the city and making more money. I turn them down. It's usually an accountant or a lawyer they send."

Cassandra grinned. "I'm an accountant by trade. Does that cross me off your list of hopefuls?"

"If it did, this would be a short conversation as you are on the short and the long list." Both of them laughed. "I want a family, Cassandra. I have some challenges but I know I can provide for a family. You know what the town thinks of me, and there will always be some small-minded person in town who will only be able to see me and say I'm a swampie. You need to be aware of that before you decide you want to be around me."

Cassandra stared at Evan. He could see her processing all of the information. He knew he had given her a lot, but before she decided to be in a relationship with him, he wanted her to know all of the issues.

"So never?"

"Never."

"Wow, that is so much more commitment than me."

Evan shook his head. "I haven't been exposed to the people or things you have. I tell you this because I want you to know what to expect if you decide to be with me."

"Is that the question?"

"Huh?"

Cassandra laughed. "You gave me all this back history because…"

Evan realized he had said everything except the question that prompted it all. "I want to try to build a tomorrow with you, Cassandra, but you need to think long and hard if you want to be in a relationship with me."

Evan watched Cassandra, but when she didn't say anything, he thought it was time to go. He stood up, and she stood with him. He had told her almost all there was to know. If she couldn't get past these—and all in all he felt this was the light news—then it didn't even make sense to bring up the other thing. His mother had told him if he couldn't let the person he hoped to build tomorrow with see him at his worst, then maybe it wasn't the person he wanted to have in his life.

"I know what I am and what I'm not, Cassandra. You are a beautiful woman and I know you must get lots of men who say they want forever. I want forever with you too. I'm just saying there are some rules for that forever, and I want you to know what they are before, or if, you give me a chance."

Cassandra reached for his hand and brought it to her cheek. Then she turned and kissed the inside of his hand.

"Usually when men approach me, they want a good time, and then one day it might become a happily ever after situation."

Evan smiled. "I'm happy to be the one to break the mold on how things are done," he whispered.

Cassandra gave him a side look. "Really? Now I'm being approached with forever from a guy who may be more decent than I am. I know I have feelings for you. I know that I want to be with someone and have a family. You've been honest enough to put it on the table for me. I want to make sure I can do the same."

Evan grinned. "Like I said, I know it's a lot to take in at once, and I wouldn't take an answer from you right now even if you thought you had one. I want you to think about it. I want you to think about us."

"It must be something big," Tom said as he took a seat across from Evan. Evan didn't say anything, he just handed Tom a glass of lemonade. Tom's wife had brought out a pitcher and put it and two glasses on the small table.

Tom eyed the glass. "I think maybe we need to get something stronger?"

Evan and Tom had been friends since boyhood. They'd grown up on the outskirts and had been each other's best friends and confidants. When Tom got married, Evan had been his best man.

"I did it," Evan said. Then he proceeded to pour himself a glass.

"Are you talking about what I think you're talking about?"

Evan nodded. "I asked her."

Tom looked at the lemonade and shook his head. "I still think we need something a little stronger, but go on."

"I told her about me being a swampie. I told her I wanted a family and that I wasn't moving," he began. He knew what Tom was waiting to hear; he wouldn't hear it, but Evan and Tom had been friends too long for him to not tell him this.

Tom put his glass down and gave Evan a stern look. "I'm not hearing everything," he said.

Evan sat back in his chair and took a long sip. "If you didn't hear it come out of my mouth, it means I didn't say it to her."

Tom shook his head. "I know you. I know you mean the best, but if you want to start out a relationship, you need to put all of your cards on the table. Not just the ones you want her to see."

Evan knew this was going to come. He knew Tom would call him on this.

"What's the point in telling everything if she can't get by the easier things?"

"You know she's not a townie. She's a city woman. I like Cassandra, and I'll admit she doesn't act like the other city women I've met. I've met good and bad just like here in Sweet Blooms. Cassandra is a cut above the best. She's not my Jessica, but she's still a good woman who has shown she's really compassionate."

Evan swallowed, then squared his shoulders. He knew this was going to be hard, but Tom was going all out.

"I'm not saying I won't tell her. I'm saying that if she can't get past the small stuff—"

Tom held up his hand. "You've always been smarter than us all. When we were growing up, you could come up with the best stories and talk your way out of most things. A lot of people underestimated you. But at the end of the day, you know what a good relationship boils down to?"

Evan nodded. "Trust."

Tom nodded in agreement. "You're asking a woman to put her life in your hands. You're promising that you're going to take care of her and any children you will have. You're giving her the keys to say something to you, and it matters to you. Both of you have to know the other one won't purposely hurt the other. How you start is how you finish. Is this how you want to start? Keeping secrets is always a bad way. It always comes out."

*Six*

The talk with Tom didn't help Evan. He tried to keep himself occupied while he waited for Cassandra to decide. He had started several pieces and actually had to toss the wood away. He wasn't seeing the wood; he was looking for an answer from Cassandra.

At night was the worst. He had time to go over what he said and how he said it. Tom's words would wash over him hourly. Evan went to Clarissa's and tried to do get some reading done with her, but he couldn't concentrate on the words or the stories.

Clarissa had talked to him the last time they had met up.

"Evan, you know I'm the last person to give anyone any kind of advice when it comes to healthy relationships, but I'm a pro when it comes to messing one up. I think you need to tell her. Don't start with secrets."

Evan had nodded and agreed, but now the time was gone, and he wasn't even sure she was going to say yes. He didn't have as much product finished as he wanted to, but at this point, if he only had one item done, he would have taken it into the store.

Evan brought in a small box and paused outside the store. There were so many doubts running through him. What if she wasn't ready? What if she had decided this was a no go, and she was trying to find a nice way to break it to him?

Someone behind him said excuse me, and Evan realized he was making trouble before it could even arrive. He took a breath and then pushed into the store. She was standing at the counter helping a customer. Her hair was down, flowing about her shoulders. She had on a white dress with black polka dots. The sleeveless dress showed off her toned arms.

"So you finally came by?" she teased.

"I wanted to have enough product in the box to justify coming in. If you said no, I could say I was here to make a drop-off. If you said yes, these would be special items to us both."

"Someone is quick on their feet," she said. She clapped her hands together and raised her eyebrows. "Let's open the box and see what memories are inside."

While she opened the box, he thought to himself that maybe this was the time to tell her the rest. When Tom and Clarissa agreed, it was definitely a universal sign of what should be done. Evan took a breath and looked at Cassandra. She was like a kid in a candy store as she took out his carvings. It was then he realized what was wrong. This was the first time he was scared to lose someone. He had been scared before, but this was different. He was scared of something he had no control over.

She looked up as if she knew he was staring at her. "Yes."

Evan's world stopped. She had said yes. He hadn't told her the rest. Now wasn't the time. He would tell her later. He would get to it before anyone else, but today, at this moment, wasn't the time.

"You're sure?"

Cassandra grinned, then leaned over the counter and pulled him close. She placed a quick kiss on his cheek.

"Yeah, I'm sure."

Evan knew he had a silly smile on his face. He didn't care. The relief was tangible throughout his body. Until now, he hadn't realized how he was holding his breath and keeping so much tension in his shoulders.

He looked around and saw the store only had one or two customers who looked like they were window shopping instead of buying goods.

"I didn't ask you before, but what about your family?" Cassandra answered. "My family isn't an issue because I'm an only child and my parents are gone, but I've heard you mention your parents in passing."

Evan watched a whole plethora of emotions cross her face.

"You know both of my parents are in business. They had hopes for me in one direction of life, but it didn't work out. I was young and wanted to please. I didn't have enough of myself yet to be able to stand up for myself."

"Would you go back to that life?"

Cassandra paused. "There have been some days when small-town life is brutal. I've got friends that I think sometimes get the short end of the stick. Then events happen and we all come together, and it blurs those times. But when the bad times are happening, I have to say I've wondered a time or two, why am I still here?

"Anyway, the way that I left made it pretty clear that I'm staying here, and I think my parents are adjusting to it even if they don't like it."

Evan heard Cassandra, but he wasn't as comfortable as he thought he would be. It would seem wrong of him to try and pin her down to what she was going to do or to ask her to make a definitive answer if she would ever go back. Plus, he still had one more thing to tell her. So he let it go. He'd address it over dinner. This was one of those times when he thought scenery and mood would help them talk about his issue.

He pushed all the thoughts out of his mind and concentrated on Cassandra. He leaned over the counter and threaded his hand into her hair and pulled her to him.

"I want to make sure you know I'm all in."

First, he kissed her on one cheek and then the other. When he looked at her, she was smiling, and then he bent down and pressed his lips to hers. Cassandra closed her eyes and reached out to put her hand behind his neck. The kiss went from chaste, to a temptation in seconds.

He wasn't sure how long they kissed, but when he pulled back, Cassandra's eyes opened slowly, and she had a smile on her face that spoke of secrets that every woman knew.

"I accept your yes."

In the background, he heard the bell go off as another customer came into the store. Then he heard a man's voice behind him.

"Excuse me, can you stop kissing my wife?"

"Cassandra Gendall."

Cassandra heard the sound of her ex, but she knew it couldn't be. She had just shared the most beautiful moment of her new life. She peered around Evan.

"Michael."

Michael stood behind Evan in a three-piece suit. Did that man ever wear anything but a full black suit? He looked amazing in it. He always had. It was one of the many reasons she had fallen for him. His hair was black with bits of grey at his temples.

How did one describe Michael Gendall? He was a force of nature. He was a CPA that had a waiting list most businesses would die for. If he couldn't fix your finances, then it couldn't be done. She knew he was in his late forties, but he had the build that easily said late thirties. At five foot eleven, he had it all—tall, dark, and handsome.

At one time in her life, she had been intrigued by him. Certainly, she had been moved by his intellect if not his looks. When they had first met, she was always amazed by his stamina and work ethic. It was definitely one of the reasons he was such a huge success in his field.

Michael stopped at the counter, and Cassandra started to touch her hair and smooth her dress. This was the way it was when he came around. He made her feel like she didn't measure up. Like there was something about her that was eternally out of place. It was a natural state of affairs after a while and a family joke that Michael would be picture perfect, and it was just a matter of finding what was wrong with Cassandra.

"So much for you being happy to see me."

Cassandra turned to Evan. Evan, who she had just promised to make a new life with.

"Evan, give me a moment to address this?"

Evan nodded and left without a word. Cassandra didn't like the look in his eye when he left. She could only deal with one thing at a time, and right now it was time to address Michael.

"Really, Michael? What would make you think I'd ever want to see you at all?"

Cassandra stopped herself from looking in a nearby mirror.

"Well, I have news. You may not be as free as you think."

"Michael, enough with the theatrics. What do you want?"

Michael pulled a paper out of his pocket and handed it to her. "You can read this and then we can decide where we would like to talk."

Cassandra was sure she didn't want to talk to him at all. She opened up the letter and read the contents. According to the document, she hadn't answered the summons in a timely fashion so they had dismissed the divorce and they were officially just separated. The decree said there was another document, and if they both signed it, the divorce would be processed posthaste.

Cassandra watched Michael look around the store. She could see him evaluating everything and putting a price on it one way or another. All of the items in the store were either useful or submitted on consignment from the local townspeople. Michael's tastes were more refined, as he would say, and nothing would pass muster with him.

"Why are you working behind a counter?" Michael asked.

Cassandra had to fight the urge to step away from the counter and give him an answer. "People who like to eat usually work. It's how they earn money and buy necessities."

Michael gave her one of his sardonic smiles. Did he practice that look?

"I understand the concept of working. I just don't understand the concept of you working, as I know you have more than enough money to never work again."

Cassandra plastered on a tight smile. "Yes, your money. I decided I'd like to earn my own money."

Michael looked around the store. "I understand you want to make a statement, but here, Cassie?"

"Please do not call me Cassie!"

"Why not? I've always called you Cassie."

Cassandra braced her hands on the countertop and looked Michael in the eye. "I have never liked being called Cassie. It rhymes with Lassie, and I don't like it."

"Don't you think that's a bit childish? Certainly, a woman of your position should be able to get beyond such silly insecurities."

Cassandra couldn't believe it. She was right back with him as if the last two years hadn't even happened. Cassandra could never win an argument with Michael. He was always right. He always knew what the right thing for the family image was. He never had a hair out of place, but she could never get all of her strands to stay in a bun.

"I see being out here with these people hasn't helped you to appreciate what you were born with," Michael said in a cold voice of disapproval.

Cassandra felt the guilt that always came. She had no defense against it. The best defense was to get through the moment quickly.

"I read the paper. You didn't have to come all this way," she said, trying to impose some reason into the conversation. "Why didn't you just mail it to me? I would have signed it."

Michael walked up to the counter and tapped his fingers on it. "I thought you would be done slumming and you'd be ready to come home."

"Home?" Cassandra said incredulously. She took a deep breath and let it out. "Listen, I'm not sure what you're doing, but there is no home for me when you are involved."

"We've been married for four years."

"Michael, we've been separated for two of those four!" she hissed.

"I know, and that is exactly my point. We've had time and separation, so we can go back to being married."

This just couldn't be happening.

"Michael, let's go over the basics. I'm the one who makes you look bad. I'm the one who can't dress appropriately. I'm the one who doesn't want to play in the circles you play. I'm the one who doesn't measure up."

Michael looked at his manicure as if he were bored with the conversation. "Cassie, you're putting words in my mouth."

"You corrected me all of the time! You'd invite my parents to join in with you."

He stopped and looked at her and then looked around the store. "Like I said before, I won't have a conversation like this out in public. I'm going to be staying here for a minute, so we can meet up later. I'm told there is only one hotel so it will be easy to find me."

"Will your clientele be able to work without you?" she said sarcastically.

"Of course not. This trip will also help them realize that and will fall in line with the rate increases that I'll be sending out."

Of course there was a plan. Of course there was an ulterior motive. Not even in his search to come and get her could he take the time to do something just for her, or to recognize what the real reason was for their breakup.

"I'll settle down and send you a time for us to meet," Michael said.

"Should I expect to get an invite from you or your E.A.?" she asked. There it was, the elephant in the room.

Michael stopped and stared at her until she started to fidget. "I don't bring my E.A.'s on personal trips."

Cassandra watched him leave, and the rage she had felt two years ago after finding out he had been cheating was still there. She didn't have a clue what she was going to do about it, though.

Michael Gendall checked into the hotel, and everything he thought about Sweet Blooms was confirmed. It was what was politely called a *quaint* town. The front desk person was someone's kid who was probably practicing for the rest of his life.

He didn't expect anything special to be prepared.

This town wasn't big enough to know who he was or that he was someone they might need one day. Today he was just a new person in town who would feed the gossip mill tonight and give the boy behind the counter something to trade and bargain with among his friends. Michael hoped the young man used the information correctly and got a good return. The young wasted these opportunities.

When Michael had gone to his room and seen the sad accommodations—a couch and a small table to hold whatever passed for breakfast—Michael went down to the bar. There were only two people at the bar—the bartender and a man with a little paunch around his middle and some thinning hair. He looked like he had seen better days. Michael didn't mind. Sitting at bars like this reminded him why he did what he did.

He motioned to the bartender to give him a beer, and he waited. It didn't take long for the man sitting at the bar to come to him.

"You're new."

Michael didn't see the need to answer the obvious.

"Did your car break down? Why did you stop in Sweet Blooms?"

Michael looked at the man and realized he wasn't drunk or incoherent, and he was curious.

"I could ask you the same thing, stranger."

The man smiled. "I'm Henry Jenkins. I'm from around here. I'm working on something with my son."

Michael held out this hand. "I'm Michael Gendall. I'm working on something with my wife."

Henry scrunched up his face. "I would know if your wife was in this town."

"Cassandra Olsen."

"Oh, I know her, but she's single. Been here two years."

"Well, I was giving her time."

Henry laughed. "I think she was giving you some time."

Michael shook his head. "You don't know her. This town isn't for her."

"Is that what she said? I've seen Cassandra. She seems pretty fine enough here in town. In fact, she looks happy. This town may not be the thing for you, but I think it was just what Cassandra wanted."

"Cassandra has more money than she can ever spend. She has a profession that puts her at the top of her game. She has a name that people would kill for."

Henry tsked and patted Michael on his back. "I'm not sure why you're here, and that laundry list you just rattled off may mean something to you, but it doesn't mean a thing to Cassandra. If you're really here to get your wife back or keep her as a friend, you might have to discover who she really is first."

Evan finally made it to Clarissa's place. Clarissa had left the back door open for him. When he walked through the back door, he was in the kitchen. True to her word, she had everything all laid out on the table.

He tipped his head. "Clarissa," he said. "Thanks for making time."

"Evan, you know it's not a problem."

She went to the stove and put on a pot of coffee. Evan took a seat at the table and waited. A few moments later, she came back to the table with a cup for each of them.

"Do you have any more contracts to look into?" she asked. Evan had left a message saying the council was going to be meeting and that he would need to hand out a summarizing document.

"No, I'm all good until Robert comes back from his trip. When he gets back, he'll take care of the contracts, and there won't be an issue. I'm hoping that any other interactions that I have to have with Ms. Waters will be verbal."

"You should be fine. Waters has expressed to the board that she will contact you if she has any further requests. I'm sure you'll be able to manage that."

Evan looked at the table and saw the piles of papers.

"Evan, you need to tell her."

He knew it wasn't going to be long before this came up, but he didn't have the answer. "I keep telling myself I need to do it."

"I'm hearing the right words coming out of your mouth but no commitment behind them."

"I'm not sure it's the right time. Cassandra is still deciding if she'll be with me."

"You're wrong, Evan."

He looked up from his papers and into Clarissa's accusing face. "What would you have me do?"

"Tell her the truth!"

Self-doubt ran through him as he thought about doing what it was that she was asking.

"You're a creative, talented guy," Clarissa praised.

"Yeah, just not a smart one."

"Stop. Not being able to read has nothing to do with being smart."

"Really? How do you think that's going to work? Hi, Cassandra, I'd like you to spend forever with me, but I can't read. I'm not sure if it's because I didn't attend school regular-like or if I have a medical condition."

"You make this more than it needs to be," Clarissa said. "You're talking out of both sides of your mouth. That I know about all too well. You're telling her you care about her, but then when it comes time to share and tell her everything, you hold back. You don't need me to do this. Ask her."

Evan knew what the problem was. It was shame. He knew what the town called him. He understood that to some, no matter what he did, and no matter how much he helped them, he would always be a swampie, someone who lived on the outskirts of town. To have to tell Cassandra, on top of it all, that he couldn't read, that he would need her to read and write all of the contracts and agreements to him, made him feel less.

He had known Clarissa for a while, and she had taught him some words, but it was slow going. He wasn't always in town, and she didn't come out to the outskirts. Now that he was here in town, he wanted to try to get some more time with Clarissa without alerting Cassandra.

# Seven

"I hear she's still married," the woman whispered to her friend.

Cassandra was in the aisle next to them. She had been restocking the bottom row, so they easily missed her. It was good to know that the rumor mill was alive and well in Sweet Blooms.

She couldn't tell who they were, but the conversation was close to what she expected today.

"Well, I hear she has money. Imagine that, the way she's dressed," said the woman.

"I don't know. I think she's dressed pretty fine. She's young. You know these young people think ripped, old, and tattered clothing are in style."

"Hmph! Are you defending her? She was going on with Evan when her husband showed up! I think Skye is going to have to find someone else to run the store. I mean, who would want someone who is married and doesn't tell anyone?"

The other woman walked along the aisle. "I don't know. I think we need to wait and see. Ever since we started marketing for people to come to Sweet Blooms, I feel like we get more than a little excitement."

The bell over the door rang. Cassandra knew she was going to have to get up and then they'd see her. She was about to stand when the women started talking again.

"Oh, it's Evan. Poor boy, falling for that married woman."

"Would you stop? We don't know anything."

"Well, even you have to admit it doesn't look good. And he's already a swampie. How can he compare to the likes of her husband?"

"Come on, let's not be rude. Hello, Evan."

Cassandra heard them move away and she let out a breath. When she heard them talking to Evan, she stood up, and everyone turned towards her. She hoped they believed she came from the storage area.

The women tittered and waved at her. As she got closer to the counter, they said their goodbyes and left.

Evan smiled at her. "I take it you know those nice women?"

Cassandra could see he was teasing now and she responded in kind.

"Those nice women, as you call it, were so busy gossiping that they didn't notice I was in the aisle right next to them."

"Were they talking about anything important?"

"They were speculating on if Skye would fire me and if I was stringing you along."

Cassandra stopped. "We didn't discuss this, and I know it will seem the height of hypocrisy for me to bring this up, but you're not dating, are you?"

The smile fell from his face, and he stared into her eyes. "I take my commitments seriously. I'm not dating.

I told you yesterday, and the words still hold for me today. You're the only woman I'm interested in."

"Okay."

Evan let the words hang between them before he asked his question. "Any update on the man who was here yesterday?"

"I'm working on helping him leave."

"Do you need help?"

For a second Cassandra thought about Evan and Michael together. Evan might bodily pick up Michael while Michael recorded the event with his phone and called a lawyer. Her absolute horror must have shown on her face because Evan reached out to her.

"Hey, I'm kidding."

Cassandra blew out a breath. "Listen, I'm going to meet with him today and get it squared away. Are we okay?"

"Yes, we're okay," Evan said. "I'm not leaving as long as you want to do this."

Cassandra smiled. "Yes, more than ever."

Michael had finished his appointments and decided it was a good time to see Cassandra. They had scheduled time this afternoon. She had said that would work because she had to do some inventory, but he was sure what they needed to talk about was more important.

He opened the door to the store, and that annoying bell went off. He didn't know how Cassandra lived with it. He walked in, and instead of seeing Cassandra behind the counter, he saw another woman who was young with dark hair and a pleasant smile.

"Can I help you?"

"I'm Michael Gendall. I'm here to see my wife."

The young lady cocked her head to the side and gave him a confused look. "I'd love to help you, but there haven't been any women in the store this morning as it's still early."

Michael tensed up and tried again. "Cassandra Olsen. She's been working here as Cassandra Olsen."

The other woman's mouth formed a perfect 'O'. "You're Michael Gendall. Let me get her; she's doing inventory."

Michael waited as the young woman went to the back. Cassandra came out, and she was dressed in jeans with a short sleeve shirt. Her hair was up in a sloppy knot, and she looked as though she might have a pen mark on her face.

"Michael," Cassandra said. "I thought we were going to meet this afternoon."

"That was the original plan. However, I had an opening, and I came over so we could take care of our appointment sooner rather than later."

"I'm working. Remember how you were always so insistent that I finish what I started? Well, I've started inventory, so this is not a good time for me."

"I'm sure anyone can do the inventory. My hourly time is probably worth more than the inventory."

"If you two will excuse me, I have customers," the young woman said as she walked away.

"Michael, that's my boss. Her name is Skye, and I have to get the inventory done before the afternoon shipment. So you can stay here if you want, or you can take a walk and come back, but I can't accommodate you right now."

Cassandra turned and walked into the back. For the first time, Michael was speechless.

"Cassie?" he called in a low whisper. Michael stood there a few moments as it sunk in; she was not coming back.

The young woman called Skye came over to him after she had rung up her customer.

"I'm sorry you came down. The inventory has to get done, and I'm the only one to man the front of the store."

Michael nodded. "Thank you for the explanation."

He walked out of the store and onto the street. Michael had decided to take Cassie up on her suggestion. Certainly a town like this had a coffee shop.

Michael Gendall had not grown up in a nice neighborhood like Cassie. He was from a different neighborhood on the wrong side of the tracks. He couldn't imagine giving up what he had to be in this town. To be a nobody, or even worse, just like everyone else. He was almost ready to go back to the hotel when he got a tap on his shoulder.

"Hello, I'm Hannah Jenkins, fiancée to Adam Cade, the millionaire. Do you think you have time for me?"

Michael looked at the bold woman with dark hair and nodded.

"If you'll lead the way, Ms. Jenkins, I'll be sure to follow you."

They walked down the block to a small coffee shop. It looked packed to Michael, and he thought they were going to have to go somewhere else. Then Hannah raised her hand and took them to an empty table towards the back.

Once they were seated, Hannah smiled at him and began. "Cassandra is a friend of mine and I would like to know why you're here."

Michael stared at Hannah and realized that he had been side kicked by a little woman. In seconds, his respect for Ms. Jenkins jumped by leaps.

"Is there a reason I should tell you why I'm here for Cassandra?"

"You don't have to. However, I'm sure you and my fiancé work in the same circles, and he likes for me to be happy. All I've gotta say is a strange man came into town to talk to my friend and he didn't make me happy. I'm sure it could negatively affect your business relationship."

Michael sat back and considered his options before he answered. "Cassandra and I are still married. I came here to offer her her old life back."

A waitress came and brought two coffee cups. The waitress didn't ask his order; instead, she left just as quickly as she came.

"She won't be back. She brought you what I was having, and she thinks you'll like it."

Michael smiled and toasted her with the coffee cup.

"Michael, may I call you Michael?"

"Please."

"I don't know that Cassandra wants to leave. If she didn't come back, you could have just sent the document for her to sign."

"I know it may not seem like it to you, but I do miss Cassie. She's an amazing woman."

"She's an amazing friend. More importantly, she's one of the town members. The whole town has adopted her as one of their own, and we are very protective."

"I can see. I'm not here to cause a problem, but I want to be given a chance. You could get your husband to move me out of town. I just want a couple of days to see if she wants to come back or not. If she says she doesn't, I'll sign and leave her to this new life."

Cassandra finished doing the inventory. When she came up from the basement, Skye was waiting there for her with some wet wipes. The inventory had been massive. Things had to be reorganized. On inventory week, she didn't even bother going to the gym. She would be sore for the next couple of days.

After she had taken the wipes and was downing her second bottle of water, Skye spoke.

"Someone is waiting for you."

Cassandra remembered Michael and let out a huge sigh. "I had hoped he would go back to the hotel. I guess he's gotten better with patience."

Skye smiled. "Oh, that wasn't who I was talking about."

Cassandra got up from the table and walked out to the front. Leaning against the counter was Evan. That smile had to be the undoing of many a teacher when he went to school. Men like Evan helped women remember the magnetic allure of a true man. She was focused on his mouth as memories of their first kiss came back to her. Would he kiss her again?

"Are you free?" he asked as he moved towards her. "I know you had to meet with —"

"That meeting didn't happen. It turned out he had a scheduled break and I didn't. When I told him to come back, he didn't. So, I'm free."

"You don't want to call him?"

Cassandra blew a strand away from her face. "You don't understand. He wants to do things in his own time. I told him that this afternoon would be great. What does he do instead? He showed up this morning."

"Sounds like you two talk at each other all the time."

Cassandra got ready to explain how Michael never listened when Evan's words started to sink in. She looked at him and laughed.

"Okay, smarty pants Evan, you're right, we do talk at each other a lot. He says he wants to talk, but the things he wants to do are so contrary to the person that I know."

Evan listened to her and didn't say a word.

"You don't want to listen to anything about him and me." What made it so bad for Cassandra was that she wanted to talk about Michael. She wanted to talk about Michael to Evan. She wanted Evan to know there were no taboos that couldn't be discussed. She didn't want their plans for a relationship to be interrupted by Michaels's appearance.

Then Evan interrupted her thoughts.

"I wonder if you know that when you're thinking on something really hard, your brow furrows and your eyes kind of go squinty."

"What?"

"I'm just saying that is obviously one of your tells. Let me try to help. Stop focusing on thinking so hard on some topics. They will work themselves out."

"Work themselves out? That does not sound very definitive to me."

Evan walked around the counter and pulled Cassandra into his arms.

"Let me answer all of the questions that I see flashing across your face. Nothing has changed between us. I still care for you. You will still have to be okay with staying in Sweet Blooms, and I think a good run for us will be if we can act as a couple for a week, doing all the things that I think we will be doing as a couple."

She knew she must have looked worried when Evan pulled away from her. "What does that mean?"

"I can't tell you if it will take the whole week, but what I can say is your happiness is the most important thing to me."

She could feel the heat coming to her eyes and the tears getting ready to flow. She didn't want Skye to see her like this. She had already received a call last night from Hannah. She knew her friends loved her, but they could be a little much sometimes. Seeing her in distress in public would travel like wildfire. "We'll meet up tomorrow?"

"I'll meet you at your house."

Cassandra watched Evan leave.

"That man looks good coming and going," whispered Skye.

Cassandra turned with a smile on her face to see Skye leaning against the doorway. "You already have a love of your life."

Skye sighed. "It's true, but it doesn't mean I can't appreciate."

Both women laughed, and Cassandra was glad she had friends in town.

# Eight

Evan waited for Cassandra on the porch just as he said he would. He thought this would be the best place to avoid the prying eyes at work.

He wanted them to start off right, and he had just finished a gift he hoped she would like. This time she would know the significance of the gift and have the choice to accept or deny it. He didn't mind giving her gifts. Especially items he had made. When she liked the things he made with his own hands, the gift did double work.

He had been listening to the gossip for the last couple of days. Between little tidbits he'd picked up here and there, he was able to get some information. He loved going to the library since they had installed the voice search ability for the blind. He'd found out that his Cassandra was very well-to-do. Michael was indeed a well-to-do CPA who commanded a big paycheck.

After doing his research, he decided he was going to appeal to the Cassandra he knew. At the end, this would all be decided by the kind of life Cassandra wanted to live. Evan made the decision not to demonize the other life because, frankly, he just didn't know it.

Instead, he would show her the world he knew and loved. And it all started with a gift.

He watched her pull into the driveway, and when she stepped out of her car, she looked beat. He knew that even though the fair was gone, there were still busloads of tourists coming in and would until the weather turned cold.

Cassandra lifted her head and saw Evan. "Evan, I'm sorry I forgot we were supposed to meet up," she said.

"I come bearing a gift." Evan held out the gift.

Cassandra looked at the gift. "I see you're pulling out all the stops."

Evan smiled. "It's true, I am. I also wanted you to know what it would be like to be with me."

"Random gifts." Cassandra gave a huge grin. "I can definitely see this as being a plus."

She opened the gift.

"Oh my goodness! This is amazing! Thank you so much, Evan."

Evan watched her run her hands over the abacus. He knew she was an accountant and she didn't have any of the other hobbies other women may have. She went to museums; he knew that because her friends were more than happy to help him. After talking to them, he started carving.

He saw the smile on her face fall away and watched her caress the abacus. Something was taking her joy, and if he read it correctly, she was about to tell him.

"Evan, maybe we should stop," she said.

"We should stop doing business?"

Cassandra shook her head. "No, I'm not talking about business. I'm talking about our relationship."

Evan thought about Michael, and he braced himself.

He knew this was a possibility, but it still hurt when he heard it.

"I take it that you changed your mind and you'll be leaving."

"No, not that. I just think I need to fix this Michael thing, and I don't want to bring any more negative attention to you."

Evan gave a chuckle. "Cassandra, I don't think there's anything you could do that will make the people in town stop gossiping. So, what's the real problem?"

"Nothing is ever simple with Michael. I want to be with you, but I think I should get rid of Michael and —"

"Listen to me, Cassandra, we will always have something happening. Hopefully it won't be another Michael, but no matter what it is, we will have to face it. We won't have the opportunity or chance to walk away from it."

Cassandra looked at Evan and began to blink her eyes. "You're a good person, Evan, and—"

He stepped up to Cassandra and tucked a strand of her hair behind her ear. "I'm not perfect. I have problems, and you'll be a part of that as well. You're just going through it first. I'll show you how it looks when I stand next to you."

"Evan, I'm scared."

"I know. I just want you to know you don't have to be scared alone. You don't have to change because I want you just the way you are."

Cassandra sniffed and looked at the abacus. "How can I say no to that, and a man who brings me an abacus?"

"You can't, so maybe we should go in instead of giving your neighbors more things to talk about?"

They both went upstairs, and Cassandra sat down and played with the abacus. "I could play with this all night long."

Evan looked at her and again remembered why he cared about her. She had the innocence of a child when she was engaged. When she played with the items he created, she didn't realize how much it brought him joy.

"I know you're distracted right now, but I told you we'd start to doing things together so you'd get an idea of what it's like for us to be together."

"Does this mean I have to stop playing with my gift?"

"No, you don't."

Cassandra looked up at him. "If I can play with this then yes, we can."

"Well, sit down, and I'll make some dinner for us both."

"You're going to cook?"

"Yes, Cassandra, I can cook. My mother taught me."

Cassandra laughed. "My mother taught me how to order out and find 24-hour diners."

"How about you play with your gift, and I'll cook."

Cassandra looked at Evan. "Will you always be doing the cooking?"

Evan smiled. "No, I won't. Eventually you'll be cooking."

Cassandra's head popped up. "Whoa, hold up there! I just told you I don't cook."

Evan started moving around her kitchen. "Fortunately for you, I'm a great teacher. It's a rule in a relationship that I share all that I know with you."

"You have rules for this relationship?"

"I like rules. I like routines."

"I should confess that I like to break the rules. I

think it comes from so many years of living with my parent's rules."

He went to her and stood in front of Cassandra. Cassandra looked up, confused. "Yes, Evan?"

He leaned down and placed a kiss on her nose. "We'll only keep the rules we both agree on. I don't want you to think I'm like your parents. We do things together, or we don't do them at all."

He was about to give her another kiss when they were interrupted by the intercom.

Cassandra jumped, and her head hit his nose. "I'm so sorry."

Evan laughed and rubbed his nose. "You've got company."

Cassandra went to the window and looked out, then came back to look at his nose. The intercom went off again.

"Is there a reason you're not answering it."

She looked at him with pursed lips, and her arms crossed over her chest. "It's Michael. He always thinks his time is so valuable. Maybe when I don't come down right away, he'll just go away."

Then the both of them heard Michael calling her name from below.

"Cassie? Cassie, are you in there?"

"Cassie like L—" Evan started.

"Abacus or no, if you finish that sentence we are going to have some words, mister."

He held his hands up and grinned.

After five minutes they both heard the car go away.

Cassandra turned to Evan who had already pulled out pots and pans to make dinner.

"I really want Michael to just go away."

After putting his hand over the skillet, he pulled out some garlic and began to peel it. "You can't avoid him forever." Evan found some oil and put a little bit in a skillet as well.

"I think it's better if I do. He'll go away just the same way he did right now."

"The question isn't should you do it but what would it get you if you did."

"Nothing. It would just be prolonging a problem. Okay, I know I have to deal with him, but I don't want to talk about him right now."

"Fair enough. Let's talk about when we will be able to make time to be with each other."

"It doesn't seem odd to talk about being together, knowing the man who is my husband was just here?"

Evan smiled. "We've got this. This is a temporary problem. That's another rule. If you come up with a solution for something, by the very nature of coming up with a solution we have taken it out of the worry category, and we move on until we find that solution doesn't work. Even then we don't worry; we just come up with a new solution."

Cassandra went back to playing with her abacus. "Okay, I'll put it out of my mind since my solution is to meet him tomorrow, sign the papers, and then get him out of town."

Evan had texted Cassandra to pick up a steak. He was happy to she had bought the steak and he took it out and began to season it.

"Good, we have a plan. Give me a few minutes. I'll make you a plate, and we can go over what our schedules look like for the next few weeks so I'll be able to plan better."

Evan wanted to make sure everything was taken care of when it came to his future. His future and Cassandra's. He had a conversation with Sandra Waters, and they had come to an agreement. He would help her build up the community center by building a new look for it, and she would be able to attract the same, if not more, people to her place. Adam had already approved it, and he had put Evan in charge of organizing it while Robert was out of town.

Evan had already decided who he was going to put on the project. He just needed to get them together so they could make it work. He hadn't had a lot of opportunities to meet with Katherine, the one who had been assigned to help out with the project, but Robert and Adam gave her glowing recommendations. Adam said he had already let her know she'd be working with him.

Today he had called her in so he could let her know about the person she'd be working with in two weeks. He met her at the Cade ranch. He was let in, and he found her in the kitchen drinking tea. She was a petite woman. If he hadn't seen her work, he might mistake her for a woman who was in fashion of some sort. Her blonde hair was in a bun, and she was pleasant to look at. Not as pretty as his Cassandra, but he knew he was biased.

"Thank you for meeting me today, Ms. Lowell," Evan said as he walked in and shook her hand.

"It's no problem, and please call me Katherine. Sweet Blooms has taken all of the formality out of business deals."

"Well, I'll get right to it. I spoke to Sandra Waters, and Adam has agreed to help her out by giving her the grant to do some renovations on the building. I need someone to help watch those costs. My input will be only about the classes and what kind will be held in which parts of the building. The designing and building will be handled by Vihaan. I think you already know him."

Katherine grinned. "I know him. He's competent. Doesn't take orders well, but I'll help him along."

Evan didn't want to touch that.

"Did you have any time restrictions? Will you have to get back to the city?"

Katherine shook her head. "No, I'm good. I'll draw up some papers and then send them to you."

"Actually, can you send them to Clarissa Rogers?"

Katherine nodded. "Of course."

He could see she really wanted to ask him why, but she held herself back. With everything else that had been going on, he had forgotten that he had to do something as well. The meeting with Katherine brought it back into focus. He needed to tell Cassandra everything.

"Water is the best thing to drink when you're outside," Evan said as he passed a water bottle to Cassandra.

Cassandra looked at the bottle and shrugged. "Part of our relationship will be eating out at picnics and drinking water?"

"It's true, water will be a part of our lives, but no. Today I brought you here so we could share."

Evan had shown up for lunch. She thought they were going to the Banter House, but instead, he brought her to the park and set up a picnic. She thought it was odd because he walked by all of the picnic tables and decided to set up on the ground.

It was kind of exciting to find out what he thought would be a part of their relationship. With Evan, everything was so upfront, and it was refreshing. It was kind of exciting waiting for him to show her what their future might entail. With Michael in town and trying to get him to leave was not proving to be as easy as she thought. These moments with Evan were even more important.

Now that she was here, she was a little confused. Sharing? And they were both on the ground? He didn't say anything, and when she got ready to talk to him, he shook his head no.

She was getting antsy. If Evan didn't say something soon, she was going to have to ask him what the whole point of this was. Then he touched her knee and pointed toward the side.

On the line where the trees had gathered, there was a fawn. It couldn't have been very old and must have been sitting in the trees. A few moments later, Cassandra saw another deer come by and nuzzle the baby fawn. After checking it over and giving her and Evan a couple of once overs, she gathered her fawn, and they went on their way.

When they were gone, Evan looked back at her and said, "Sharing."

She reached over to him and hugged him. "That was amazing."

Evan laughed. "It's funny to me you're whispering

now after they've left. For a moment there, I wasn't sure you were going to make it not talking at all."

She turned to him and grinned. "I almost didn't!"

She watched as he pulled out sandwiches and salad. They talked about her day and what was going on in the store. She made a concentrated effort not to talk about Michael. This was their time, and she didn't want to spoil it. After the sandwiches, she laid down as he cleaned up.

"I want you to know I could really get used to this part. You cleaning everything up. A man cleaning up after me wasn't something I ever thought about, but now that I've experienced it, I have to ask you, was it good for you too?"

Cassandra burst out laughing. Instead of a verbal response, she felt his shadow above her. She opened her eyes just in time to see him lower his head to hers and kiss her. A moment ago she was teasing him, and the next she was lost in the kiss. He kept the kiss light by moving his lips across hers in a promising way. She turned her head to the side, angling her head so she could wrap her arms around his neck.

He continued to kiss her once her arms were anchored around his neck. He never lowered his body to touch hers, but she traced her hands over his shoulders. When she felt the heat travel along her body, she tightened her grip on his shoulders.

He pulled away and looked at her. His eyes were filled with passion and something else she couldn't name.

"Evan?"

He leaned his forehead against hers and then took a breath and pushed away from her. She opened her eyes and didn't release her grip on him. "What are you doing?"

"What's best for us both."

Cassandra was so taken aback that she let him go. "I thought…"

Evan sat back and smiled. "Don't worry, Cassandra, I believe you're worth the wait."

# *Nine*

"So how does it feel to be the object of attention for two men?" Sandra Waters asked Cassandra as she paid for her purchases. Skye was ringing up Sandra's purchases and turned to Cassandra and wiggled her eyebrows. "I didn't think you had it in you."

Cassandra had it in her alright, and right now she was thinking she wanted to give it to Sandra Waters. "It's not something I planned. Do you think I purposely left Michael?"

"I don't know. I mean, we're not in your personal life or anything," Sandra said.

"Cassandra isn't that type of woman, Sandra, and I'm surprised at you," Skye said.

Sandra put on a fake smile. "Of course. Forgive me. I'm just saying it figures that you came from the city and Michael seems very modern. It's a sharp contrast to a swampie. Oh, I mean the people who live on the outskirts."

Cassandra couldn't believe what she was hearing. She knew that Evan was rebuilding her community center and still that wasn't enough for her to forget where he came from. Having both Michael and Evan together was a feat in and of itself. She knew when people looked at him, they only saw the outside but it didn't make it any less wrong and she didn't think it hurt Evan any less.

"Well, if I had to choose between the two, there's no question who I would choose," Sandra said snidely.

Cassandra thought about letting it go and then decided not to.

"I wonder who you would choose, Sandra. I mean, Evan is rebuilding your community center at no cost to you. He's moved into town so he can make sure your classes are full and that you don't lose money. He's doing all that for you, and still, you call him a swampie. I wonder if Michael would be that forgiving towards you? Then again, we don't have to worry about you making a choice because you'd never have this kind of problem with two men anyway."

Cassandra picked up her bag and walked out of the store. She called Hannah as she left. What she needed now was a friend to talk her down.

"I couldn't believe the way she was talking about Evan after all he's doing for her," Cassandra said at lunch. "She called him a swampie and made it seem like Michael would be the better choice. I know Evan told me about the prejudice that some people have, but she's gone above and beyond."

Hannah nodded and took a chicken strip from the appetizer basket. Cassandra watched her put the strip on her plate, mix ketchup and mustard together, and then dip the strip. After a few moments, Hannah must have noticed the silence, and she looked up.

"Don't mind me."

Cassandra eyed the ketchup and mustard concoction and then nodded towards it.

"Oh! This? I picked this habit up from high school. Please don't get distracted; you were ranting about how unfair Ms. Waters was treating Evan."

Cassandra stopped. "Ranting? Was I?"

Hannah waved off her concern. "It's completely normal considering you and Evan."

"Considering?"

"Okay, let's not play coy. The reason you feel the need to defend Evan is because you two are getting closer. You're smart; let's not lose ourselves in disillusionment."

Cassandra grabbed a chicken strip. "You're right; we are getting closer." She thought about the last time they were together. Both of them sharing.

Hannah snapped her fingers to get Cassandra's attention. "Earth to Cassandra. Listen to me. I want nothing but happiness for you. But I also want to make sure you understand that Evan isn't like other guys. When he says he's all in, he's all in."

"You don't think I'm all in?"

"Well, let me say that I spoke with Michael. He thought he had a chance with you. A man doesn't usually have that thought unless there's some proof or incentive."

"I haven't given him anything, Hannah," Cassandra said, hurt that her friend wasn't on her side like she thought.

"You haven't dashed all of his hopes either. I know things aren't easy with you and Evan, but I need you to be clear on what you want to do."

Cassandra reached out and grabbed Hannah's hand. "I know what I want. I think I need to be sure he wants me."

"So here is my sage advice for you. Take care of your Michael issue. Trust Evan, Cassandra. I don't tell any woman to do that lightly. Evan is a good man."

Cassandra smiled. "I know. I want to say my head knows, but right now the rest of me needs to catch up."

Michael was ringing the intercom. He saw her car. He had already been to the store, and he knew she wasn't there. He hadn't gotten where he was without being persistent. He pressed it again and then he heard the answering static.

"Come up already."

When he opened the door, she was standing at the top of the steps. He took the steps two at a time. When he got to the top, she stepped aside for him to enter.

"Do you have the paper, Michael?"

He didn't sit but stood inside, taking his surroundings and then looked at Cassie. "You were hoping that I would give up and just leave the papers for you to sign?"

Cassie was frustrated. Her arms were folded under her chest, and she was breathing hard.

"Is it just us, or are you waiting for your boyfriend to show up?"

"Michael, please. It's just us two here. There's no reason for us to have anyone else."

She motioned for him to take a seat. The couch was quaint. He knew he was seeing the same things that

Cassie was seeing and still he knew he was missing something. "I'm so confused. Is this what you really want?"

Cassandra looked around the room, and a smile lit her face.

"Yes, Michael, this is what I really want. This is me."

"You're better than this."

Cassandra shook her head and gave him a sad look. "Why are you really here, Michael?"

"I'm here because you're my wife."

"You came back for your possession?"

Michael was confused. "What happened between us? We had it all."

Cassandra looked into her hands, and when she looked up, he saw there were tears in her eyes. "Michael, we had it all when we had nothing. When you were going to school, and I was working in a diner, we had it all."

Anger coursed through him and he shook his head. "We had nothing! We lived paycheck to paycheck. Maybe that was great for you, but it wasn't for me. I grew up with nothing. I lived with nothing. I thought you understood I wanted it all. I wanted the world to be at our feet. I wanted–"

Cassandra reached out her hand and caressed his cheek.

"Then that was the problem. The only thing I wanted was you."

Michael leaned into her hand and then kissed her palm.

"I'm sorry about Nancy."

Cassandra stood up and stepped away from the couch.

"I think you need to go."

Michael looked at Cassandra, nodded, and left. He needed to think. He needed to reorganize. He needed to find out what he was going to do.

# Ten

"It was sad," Cassandra said as Evan put rice on the plates. "I never knew how far apart we were in our thinking."

Evan sat across from her at the kitchen table and passed her a bottle of water. This was another night of him cooking for her. When Cassandra had called him, her voice said he needed to be there right away.

"You mean you didn't know how far away you were when you were married, or today?" he asked.

"Both. We had been together for two years; you'd think I would have been able to see the differences. I mean, we were together while he was in school, and all through it, I thought we were fighting the good fight and fighting to be with each other. All this time he was hoping to take over the world."

Evan looked at her and shrugged as she devoured the fried chicken. "I think it's important for people to have closure in their lives. You two meeting here will give the both of you that."

Cassandra shrugged. "Maybe. I don't think Michael is looking for closure, though. I think he just wants to be right. I still wish, closure or no, that he would leave."

Evan got up and emptied the rest of the rice onto her plate. "I think right now you are of two minds. You want him to give you the papers so you can go on with your life. There is another part of you that still cares for him and hopes that he can go on and find happiness."

Cassandra stopped her fork midway to her mouth.

"You seem to be so mellow about the whole thing."

Evan thought about it. "My mother used to say that when you love someone, it never goes away. You can love more than one person in your life. Loving a person means you care about what happens to them even if they can't stay with you."

"Do you think he'll find someone? Do you think he'll be happy?"

Evan finished up the last of the food on his plate.

"I can't tell you if he will or won't. The million dollar question is, when will he give you the papers?"

Cassandra sighed. "You're right. I'll give him a call. Enough already about Michael. You have taken all this time to get me up to speed about what you'll do for me, and we almost never talk about you and what you're doing."

Evan laughed. "Well, I can tell you I'm moving the plan along. I found two people to manage the community center project."

Cassandra looked at him for a bit longer. "What aren't you telling me?"

"It's a feeling, nothing more."

Cassandra picked up the plates and put them in the kitchen sink. "I don't discount feelings. What is it?"

"Well, I knew I wanted Katherine to keep the

numbers. And I thought that I would get Vihaan to do the architecture and design."

"Okay, what's the problem?"

"When I told Katherine she would be working with Vihaan, she made a couple of comments that made me think they had some past history or they might experience some friction working together."

"Do you think it's going to be a problem to the project?"

Evan shook his head. "I think the both of them are professional enough that they can get through the project, but I have to make the decision before Robert gets back. It's a big responsibility."

Cassandra tapped the table to get his attention. "You do know you'll be fine, right? Adam and Robert wouldn't have asked you if they didn't think you could do this. More importantly, I know you can do this."

Evan smiled. "Thanks, I think I need all the support I can get with this one."

They moved from the table and went to the couch. Evan reached for the remote and Cassandra stayed his hand.

"I have to ask you a question."

Evan knew whatever it was she wanted to ask was important. "Go ahead."

"One of my biggest fears is a man cheating. Do you ever feel the urge to try something else? I mean, especially for you, it would seem that it would be understandable."

Evan looked into Cassandra's eyes and saw the hurt and pain of past betrayal. Her voice had become thin and low. He reached out and put his hand under her chin so she would look him in the eye.

"I've never had the itch, as they call it. I've never thought about it either. It took me a long time to find you, and I'm not looking for anyone else."

Cassandra smiled nervously. "This is all new to me. New starting a relationship this way. New having a preview plan."

Evan laughed. "Don't worry. We're in this together."

Cassandra laughed with him, and he couldn't stop looking at her. He was happy she had called him tonight. He thought it was a good sign as to where their relationship was going.

"Talking about relationships, let's do something that would be a big part of our downtime," Evan said.

Cassandra looked at him funny but nodded in agreement.

"Let's watch a movie," he said.

Cassandra looked at him as if he had grown another head. "On what?"

Evan smiled. "It just so happens I have my tablet with me. We can watch it on that if you don't mind sitting close."

Cassandra nodded. "I'm okay sitting close, but the real question is, what are we going to watch?"

Evan sat down with his tablet. "Fortunately for you, I have a large selection. Would you like to look at an old movie or new?"

Cassandra saw all of the movies on the tablet and looked at Evan. "It's your night. You decide. I already asked you over, and you cooked, so we can watch whatever you want."

Evan gave her a look. "Are you sure?"

Cassandra laughed. "Oh yes, I definitely want to know what you're going to choose."

"Mulan it is!"

Cassandra fell backward on the couch. "Mulan. Really?"

Evan shrugged and gave her an unrepentant grin. "Let this be a lesson to you. When offered the chance, make sure you take it. Now let's get this party rolling with Mulan!"

The rest of the day was spent arguing over the finer points of Mulan.

The next day Evan showed up with a basket to take Cassandra to lunch. She saw him walk in the door with a basket and asked, "Is this going to be another sharing moment?"

Evan smiled. "No, today it's just lunch."

Cassandra looked at Evan dressed in his jeans and t-shirt. "Well then, let's go ahead, and you can feed me."

They found a picnic table, and he laid out the spread for them both. When all of the sandwiches were on the table, he pulled out a bottle of water.

Cassandra laughed. "You were really serious about water being a part of our everyday life."

"I'm looking out for you long term."

Cassandra picked up a plate and a sandwich. "I'm not complaining. In fact, I think I could really get into this. You cook, you clean, and you come when I need you. This isn't a hard sell at all. I'm even willing to forgive you for choosing Mulan."

Evan laughed along with her. "Your compassion and understanding knows no bounds."

"Thank you, kind sir."

"Since you are getting so much from this experience, I think we will turn this into a sharing experience."

Cassandra placed her hand against her chest. "Oh, another sharing experience. What will be sharing?"

"How about you tell me one thing you like about me, and I'll do the same."

Cassandra thought about it and then nodded. "Who goes first?"

Evan shrugged. "It's not even a question. You do."

"Okay. The thing I like the most about you is your honesty. I have to say, no matter what happens, I know you will always tell me the truth."

Cassandra looked at Evan and saw his smile fade for a moment.

"Evan?"

"Thank you, Cassandra. I am happy that you have so much faith in me, but I want you to remember that we are all human. Although I'll try my best to live up to your expectations."

Cassandra stared a little longer at Evan. She could tell something was suddenly wrong but didn't know what. "Hey, stop stalling. If you think you can burn my lunch time with some deep introspective thoughts, think again. I'm waiting."

Evan's smile got wider, and he grabbed a water bottle and opened it to take a drink. "I don't know, there are so many things I could mention."

"Okay, okay, stop the stalling."

"Okay, the thing I admire about you is your strength. When I first saw you in the store, I could tell you didn't know how to work the cash register, and you were more comfortable writing up receipts. Still, no matter what was asked of you, you didn't turn away.

Then when you came to my room to look at the next items, and I saw you up front, I could see the strength in your bone structure that I had seen in your personality. Strength is what I admire about you the most."

Cassandra reached out and laid her hand open for Evan. When he placed his hand atop hers, she spoke. "Thank you. I'll remember this always. This was perfect."

"Cassie?"

Cassandra hung her head. It just couldn't be that he would show up here and now. She looked up, and sure enough, there was Michael in his suit.

"Hello, Michael."

Evan glanced towards Michael and held out his hand. "Michael," he said.

Michael didn't take his hand. Instead, he looked at his hand as if it were disgusting. "Who are you?"

"I'm Evan Sparrow."

Michael shook his hand and then took a seat next to Cassandra.

"Cassie, I think we still need to finish our conversation."

Cassandra let out a small sigh. "I don't think we have anything left to say to one another. The only thing we should discuss are papers."

"We'll get to the papers." Michael seemed fidgety and frustrated. He turned to look at Evan, who was casually drinking water. "Can I assume you are the reason that my wife finds it inconvenient for me to be around?"

"What took you so long to find her?"

"I thought she would come back. Cassie has always been headstrong and impulsive."

"If my wife left and didn't come back within the first week, I'd go find her."

Michael waved it off and shook his head. "Maybe that's how it works for you because you don't have the obligations that I have."

Cassandra listened to the men talk. This was the first time she had ever seen anyone stand up to Michael. It was unheard of, and yet here she was, watching someone do the thing she had wanted to do all the time.

"Now you have time for a wife? Will your time be taken away by something else to make you forget you have a wife?"

Michael's gaze focused on Evan. "I'm sorry, did anyone ever clear up my first question? Who are you and what are you doing with my wife?"

"I'm Evan. I thought we covered this already."

"I'm not simple. I know your name. The question is, who are you to my wife?"

Cassandra heard the question, and she wanted to know what Evan would say. They were still in the learning phase. She didn't want Michael to know she hadn't been completely claimed by Evan either. She didn't have words for it, but there was a part of her that didn't want to appear unwanted. What made it worse was she didn't have any choice in the matter at all. So she stayed quiet and looked at Evan and waited.

Evan smiled. "I'm the man who's going to marry Cassandra Olsen," Evan said.

Michael's face changed from instigator to confused. "She's still married."

"Like I said, I'm going to marry Cassandra Olsen. I wouldn't worry about it if I were you. You won't be around when it happens."

Evan said it as clear as day. Cassandra was amazed he hadn't stuttered or looked away. She wanted to know what he thought, and now she did. She knew that was his intention, but hearing it, and hearing it now, was exactly what she needed.

Michael looked at her as if he were waiting for her to contradict what Evan had said. Then he looked back at Evan and started to laugh. It wasn't what she expected. His laughter brought back all the times she had tried to do something, but he had found some way to make her feel less than and foolish. Evan asked the question she didn't have the courage to ask.

Evan finished his water bottle and placed it on the table. "What's so funny?"

"Cassie with you? You have nothing to offer her. She could buy you several times over. Why would she be with you?"

Cassandra was embarrassed by Michael's words. Was that all he thought about her? Did he think she was so shallow that those things mattered to her? Then she looked at Evan. To her surprise, he didn't even seem to be phased by what Michael had said.

"It all makes sense now," Evan said. He reached across the table and placed his hand atop Cassandra's. "You know, until you said that I didn't understand anything. Now it's all clear. You just don't know Cassandra. None of the things you mentioned really matter to her. The things that do matter to her can't be bought. She has a good heart, and she sees people for who they are. I'm sorry that you didn't get a chance to really know her at all."

Cassandra listened to Evan, and she was lost in his words. It was the first time she remembered anyone standing up for her. It was the only time she could remember someone standing up successfully to Michael. She knew that Evan had a kind heart and that he'd said those words to protect her, but for a moment she could almost believe they were true. When he spoke, his hand had grasped hers, and she had felt special and loved.

Michael kept his gaze on Evan and then shook his head as he stood up. "This wasn't what I was expecting," he said. When he was on his feet, he looked at their joined hands. "It seems there might be a bit of truth in what you say. If so, it would also follow that I'm the unwanted one here. Cassie, Evan, have a good lunch."

As Cassandra watched him leave, she noticed his shoulders weren't as straight as they normally were, and for a moment she felt sorry for him. He looked so alone.

"Thank you," she said to Evan.

"It needed to be said, and I was happy to deliver it." He reached in the basket and got another water bottle. "You have a soft heart."

Cassandra looked at Evan and shrugged.

"I remember what it was like to be alone, and I wouldn't wish that on anyone."

Evan opened the water bottle. "Sometimes we're alone because we push everyone away. When that happens, we need to grow before we can be happy."

"That's even worse."

"Why?" Evan shrugged. "If a person doesn't love themselves, they can't love someone else."

"I was already feeling bad for him, but when you say that, I know it's a life problem. I look back on the life I had with him. I tried so hard to make things work. I looked the other way when I thought he was having affairs. I wanted him to know that no matter what, I was there for him. If he was having that problem and I stayed with him, it means I had the same problem. We were two toxic people who needed help. I failed him as his wife."

Evan got up and walked around the table to sit next to Cassandra. He took both of her hands and brought them to his lips, kissing each one.

"You need to listen to me," he said sternly.

Cassandra lifted her gaze, but it was already starting to blur from the unshed tears.

"Once upon a time you were that girl," he said. "You lived in that world, and you did what they said. Then one day you made a choice. You decided to choose you. You decided to love you. At that moment, you shed all of your old habits and came to Sweet Blooms. In Sweet Blooms, you have been nothing but the strongest of women. You've been independent, you take the initiative, and you live fully. So it's true; once upon a time you were that girl, but today you are an amazing woman who owns her own choices. Own that and don't let anyone take it from you."

"Thank you," she murmured.

"We all have to find ourselves."

Cassandra sighed. "I admit I'm still feeling conflicted about him. I'm upset that he's here but I'm sad that he's alone."

"You loved him."

"This kind of love cost too much."

Evan smiled. "My mother would say all love is precious."

"Hopefully he understands now." Cassandra thought back to the conversation she and Michael had had at her apartment. "He's still working through his history. But I don't have to be a part of that process."

Evan sighed. "My last words on it are this: At one time in your life, you two did share something precious. It may not be there now, but it was there then. If you can, you should separate as friends."

"I'll think on it. Thanks for being here."

"It's where I belong."

Cassandra was going to make a comment when Evan's phone rang. When he picked it up, he stood so only he could see the caller.

"Sure, I'm on my way." When he hung up, he smiled at Cassandra and held out his hands. "I've got to go. I'm sorry."

Cassandra waved away his excuses. "Let's clean up. I'll go to the store, and you can go take care of your business."

Evan agreed, and they packed up quickly. Evan put his phone down in order to help pack the basket, and as Cassandra was picking up the garbage, she saw the message on his phone.

*Received call from Clarissa.*

She would wait and ask Evan later what Clarissa was calling him about and why he had to go see her.

*Eleven*

"Would you like to explain this to me?"

Evan looked around the temporary office. It was set up behind the community center. Katherine had decided to visit the site a week early to see where she would be working. Evan could see how this was not what anyone had thought it would be.

Sandra Waters was responsible for providing space for Katherine and Vihaan. She left a note explaining that all of the rooms in the center were being used to generate revenue and couldn't be used for office space. So she set up a temporary shelter outside the center in the back of the building.

Katherine had her hair up in her normal knot, and her eyes were blazing with indignation. "Did you know she was going to do this, Evan?"

She didn't even wait for him to answer. "I get she wants to make money, but was this the only option? I can't imagine there being no office space in this town. What could I have done to deserve this? Adam told me I could go ahead and get the office set up. What office? This is a tin can, and I don't even see any air conditioner.

I'm going to kill Adam and hide his body on one of his own sites."

Evan listened to Katherine fuming in the shed, and he couldn't help but grin. As if things couldn't be bad enough, the facilities, such as they were, were located in the back of the shed.

"I don't think the project will run long at all," Evan tried to help.

Katherine turned on him like a rattlesnake. "You don't think the project will run long," she said in a sweet, candy-like voice. "Well, let me tell you about projects. They always run long. They have problems. Problems pop up, like unexpected items that everyone thought we agreed on but it turns out no one planned for, and all of that happens even when we're organized and on the same page," she said through clenched teeth.

"I realize this is a shock. Why don't you come into the center and we'll see what we can do," Evan offered.

Katherine glared at him for a moment more then followed him into the center. He took her into the lounge and got her a cup of coffee.

"I think if we can talk to Sandra Waters, we can try to kick around some other alternatives," Evan said as he tried to appease her.

Katherine didn't say anything. Instead, she took a sip of the coffee and closed her eyes. When she opened her eyes, she pinned Evan with her stare.

"Evan, I know you've lived here all of your life, but I have to tell you as a person who was born and raised in the city, there is something off in small towns. Maybe you're immune to it because you were born here, but to the rest of the world, small towns are just horror movies waiting to happen. I'd take a dark city street any time."

Evan laughed. "I'm confused. Are you angry with the space or angry that you need to stay in Sweet Blooms?"

"My answer to minimizing the things that could go wrong is to keep things as standard as possible. I would like to be in an office, in a building. Being put in a shed seems like I'm asking for something weird and untoward to happen to me."

"You do know this is Sweet Blooms. Until Adam came, no one even knew we existed."

Katherine pointed her finger. "You see! Who lives like that?"

"It's cozy. Give it a chance and it will grow on you," Evan said.

Katherine placed her hands around her cup. "Probably, but the problem is that fungus grows on you also. You never hear anyone advocating for that."

Then the door to the lounge opened up and in came Sandra Waters. Her gaze fell on Evan first and then Katherine.

She came forward with her hand extended. "I'm Sandra Waters."

Evan cleared his throat. "I'm sorry, I thought you two had already met. Ms. Waters, this is Katherine –"

Katherine interrupted him. "I'm Katherine, the cost manager of the community center project."

The women shook hands, and Evan wondered if there was a way for him to escape.

Sandra had on what could only be kindly called a fake smile.

"Oh, well, I'm surprised to see you in here in the lounge area for the instructors."

Katherine's voice became sweeter. "Oh, really? Is there a rule I'm not aware of?"

Sandra laughed. "Of course not. I just thought it would be too much of a journey for you and your team to have to come in here. Maybe I can buy you a coffee machine to help make your new accommodations a little friendlier."

Evan could feel the tension in the room, and he was about to intervene when Katherine spoke.

"You know that won't be necessary. I'm sure we will all adjust as soon as the project starts."

Sandra nodded her head in satisfaction and left the lounge. Katherine swallowed the rest of the coffee and then stood up.

"You see what I mean, Evan? Only in small towns do people try to exert their authority over the person who holds the purse strings on their project. Leave it all the way it is. When I come back in two weeks, I'll straighten it then."

Evan watched her walk out of the room and shook his head. He would never get women. Thank goodness he only needed to be concerned about one.

Cassandra thought about her life and all that Evan had said. It was time to clear up her past so she could go forward with her future. Cassandra hoped this evening would be about healing and not pity. The reason why was moot now. The fact of the matter was, she had invited Michael over and told him to bring the paper with him.

She wanted to keep everyone in the present and try not to dwell on the past. In the past, she always lost one on ones with Michael. She let out a breath and settled down. She could do this. She wasn't Cassie anymore.

When the intercom rang, it broke her out of her rah-

rah chant, and for a split second she thought about why living on the second floor was a horrible thing. She had originally been on the first floor but had to move while they were doing necessary renovations. She rang the intercom, and she could hear Michael coming up the stairs. She didn't wait for him to knock. Instead, she decided to do something proactive, and she went to open the door.

"Hi Michael," she said, stepping aside to let him in. She was temporarily speechless because Michael had on jeans and a polo top.

"Cassie."

She didn't even know Michael owned a pair of jeans. These jeans were black, with a burgundy polo top tucked into them. She was glad that she had ordered in and that she had put on jeans herself. In the back of her mind, she heard Evan's voice telling her, "If nothing else, you should be able to be friends."

Michael followed her to the kitchen table in her eat-in kitchen. He looked at the Chinese boxes and raised an eyebrow. "I see we ordered in."

"Yes, I did. I didn't want to have to rush home after work and work again." Cassandra waited for the criticism on how it shouldn't have been any work at all.

"I thought you enjoyed cooking," he said idly.

Cassandra stopped and looked at him. "I thought you enjoyed a home cooked meal."

Michael smiled. "Maybe we should have talked more. I always prefer to go out."

Cassandra pulled out paper plates and real forks. He looked at the selection she had given him.

"Cassie, how does this make sense?" he said with a smile.

Cassandra looked at the plates and forks and then at Michael. "If we're going to make it through this evening, I need you to not call me Cassie."

He looked at her for a moment and then nodded. "If it really disturbs you, then yes, I'll call you Cassandra."

"Thank you. The plates and forks make perfect sense. I want to throw away the plates that held the food, but I want to make sure I can actually pick up the food, so I need real utensils."

"As you wish."

He set the table for them both and then they sat down. As she got ready to sit down, she was extra happy that she had ordered. The evening would have a nice flow to it as long as the food was already done. No uncomfortable silences. Instead, they served the food out onto the plates and ate.

Michael was the first one to break the silence. "Why did you pick Sweet Blooms?"

Cassandra smiled. "Because the guy changed my car oil for free. I figured he was nice even though I had just met him. I wanted to meet the rest of the town to see if they were just as nice."

"And I guess you found them all to be nice?"

Cassandra thought about it. She thought about how people treated Evan. "I think the town is like any other place. You have your good, and you have your bad."

"Don't you miss traveling?"

Cassandra popped another dumpling in her mouth as she thought about it. "No, I don't. There's a lot going on in this small town."

"I looked into your account. You haven't touched any of your money. Did you hate me so much you would live in squalor?"

Cassandra put down her fork and looked at Michael.

"So, let me get this straight. The only reason I would have not to touch that money was that I hated you? I don't hate you, Michael. I don't like you all the time, but I don't hate you. I just wanted to make sure I knew how to take care of myself."

"I thought it was my job to take care of you."

"Fulfilling your duty doesn't mean you're taking care of a person."

"I see that now."

Cassandra was wondering what she had been thinking when she thought this up.

Michael had put down his plate and fork. "Why didn't you go back to being a CPA? It's what you knew, and you're good at it."

Cassandra looked at Michael and smiled. "Thanks. That's the first time you've actually said that."

"What?"

"That I was good at being a CPA."

Michael looked at her as if she had grown another head. "I'm sure I must have said it many times."

"Oh, really?"

"Yes."

"Fine, try to recall one time."

"I'm sure there must have been —"

Cassandra shook her head. "No, not one time. As to why I didn't open up as a CPA, I wanted to do something where I got to talk to people every day, and they weren't scared. Every time someone comes to a CPA, they're in trouble or trying to stay out of trouble. In either case, it's not a happy one."

"I never looked at it that way. I always thought

people came to me when they needed help only I could provide, and it was enough."

The meal was about done. There were some new points that were brought up. They cleaned up the table and threw out whatever they didn't eat or what was left on the plates.

"I want to thank you for coming. I know the last couple of days have been stressful. If they haven't been stressful for you, they have been for me."

"It wasn't my intention," Michael said in a low voice.

"Did you bring the papers?" she asked.

Michael's eyes widened and then closed. "Yes, I brought them."

There was a sense of anticipation now that she knew he had the papers on him. She'd thought he would come up with some other excuse why he couldn't bring the papers. Michael would always be that go-getter; it was bred in him. She wasn't built that way.

"Are you and Evan really an item?"

All of Cassandra's alerts went off. Had she been taken again by the master?

"Evan and I have been seeing each other," she said, not wanting to tell him about the bracelet. She unconsciously touched the bracelet on her wrist.

"How did you two meet?"

"Do you really want to know, and does it really matter?"

"I really want to know. I'm here tonight, Cass… Cassandra. I brought your papers. I'm still concerned about you."

"He's an artist, and we met through the store. He's one of our biggest sellers at the store. I don't know if you know, but Adam Cade from Cade Designs decided to come home. He's from Sweet Blooms. He asked Evan to head the woodworking shop here, and Evan will be giving classes at the community center as part of some deal with the board."

Michael leaned back. "For a man who is doing so much, there isn't much information on him."

"Really, Michael? You had someone look him up?"

"I'd like to say I didn't, but I did. I looked up the whole town before I came so I would know what I was walking into. Evan's part of a group that there is little to no information on. If I hadn't met them, I would have said they were some kind of secret cell."

Cassandra smiled. "Well, rest assured, he is not part of a secret cell. If anything, he's what you'd call averse to society. I'm sure you know that since gossip is quicker than the news in small towns. Evan and his family used to live on the outskirts of town."

"It seems like he's an outsider in a group that is already insular. I want you to make sure you're okay. I would never have thought that you'd be his type of woman."

Cassandra shook her head. "You've been here less than two weeks, and you know what kind of woman he would want?"

Michael shrugged his shoulder. "I admit I could be wrong, but I'm bringing it up because I don't want you to get hurt."

Cassandra took a deep breath and then let it out. "Listen, why don't we get to the papers?"

Michael nodded. "I really don't see why you're so upset over this since I'm just trying to be helpful."

"Michael, maybe I don't think it's very helpful for you to tell me that I'm not the right kind of woman for the man I'm currently seeing, and plan on marrying."

Michael pulled out the paper from his jacket that he'd worn over and gave it to her. She put it down on the table and signed it.

Michael looked it over and then signed it. "I'll get it filed, and they will send you your official copy in the mail when it has been finalized."

Cassandra stood with her arms wrapped around her. "I don't think there's anything else for us to discuss. Maybe it would be better if you just left."

Michael stiffened. "I'm not sure why you're so angry. When I try to talk to you, I'm the bad person."

"Right now you're not talking to me, you're finding fault in me, and I don't need that in my life anymore."

Michael picked up his jacket and went to the door. Then he turned around and looked at her.

"What now, Michael?" she asked exasperatedly.

"Your bracelet has been bothering me all night. I know I've seen it before."

Cassandra held out her wrist. "This bracelet? It's one of a kind."

Michael shrugged his shoulders. "It might be rare, but it's not one of a kind. I saw it on a woman who was asking me more information about my taxes than my tax lawyer did. What was her name? Candy, no. Caroline, no. It was…"

"Was it Clarissa?" Cassandra asked.

Michael smiled. "Yes, it was. I'm glad you knew because you know those things drive me crazy. Anyway, thank you for dinner. I'll be in town for a couple of more days if you want to talk."

"Thank you, but I don't think so." Cassandra closed the door and leaned against it, only to slide down until she hit the floor. Shame and foolishness flooded her system.

Was she wrong?

Was it happening again?

She had never asked Evan about the call, and now there was the bracelet. Was she destined to always find men who couldn't be faithful to her?

# Twelve

Evan was done with his latest creations. It had taken him an hour to wait for the linseed oil to dry on the carvings. It had taken him two days to do the paintings. These pieces were all princess pieces. He'd become inspired after watching Mulan.

He'd packed all of the items, and his mood was upbeat. He hoped that Cassandra would look at the pieces and she'd remember the time they had spent together. When he walked into the store, he searched for her, wanting to see her reaction. She was behind the counter ringing up a customer's purchases. She didn't seem like her happy self. He hoped when she saw the pieces it would brighten her day.

He walked to the counter and cleared his throat. When Cassandra looked up, her smile fell away, and he saw her take a breath. Evan wasn't sure what had happened, but whatever it was, he wanted to fix it.

"Hey," he said, feeling awkward for some reason.

Cassandra wouldn't even look him in the eye. "Evan, can we talk outside for a moment?" she asked.

"Of course."

He left the box on the counter and then waited until

she had finished with the customers. Cassandra called over her shoulder, and Skye came out. After that, Evan followed Cassandra out of the store. She walked a few steps to the side, so they weren't blocking the door, but they were still on the same block as the store.

There was a sense of dread about Cassandra. Evan didn't know what was wrong, but he was happy they were going to work through it. He thought things were better between her and Michael. Evan tried to think of all of the things it could be and came up with nothing. The good news was she had reached out.

Cassandra ran her hand through her hair and let out a breath. "I've been thinking on everything," she started. "I know you've been putting in a lot of time and effort."

Evan smiled. "Of course. I think it's important when you're starting things to put in the right amount of time."

Cassandra nodded and seemed to become more aloof. "Yes, it's important to start things off right; otherwise they'll never be the way they are supposed to. I think it's been very informative, but I think it's time to face facts and end this."

He looked at her and tried to rationalize what was happening. "When did you come to this conclusion?"

"It's really not a question of when I came to the conclusion. The thing that I should have considered is that we're just too different. You've gone out of your way to explain how things are here, though."

"I don't have an issue with talking to keep the air clear."

Cassandra cleared her throat and took a small step back when he finished saying that. He didn't understand what was going on. He was making long term plans with her. He had dreams that already included her. He knew there was something between them that was more than just physical attraction. They had trusted each other to speak plainly. He thought they were at the place where he could tell her everything, and now this.

He was sure of his feelings, and he thought she was too. If only she would give him some reason as to why things were changing.

"I think I want us to be friends, and above all, I want to say thank you," she finished.

"Be friends? Thank you? You make it sound like we had a business deal," he bit out. "Tell me what happened. You owe it to us to tell me what I did wrong."

Cassandra stopped and looked him in the eye. "I don't owe you anything."

"Then what were we doing? What was I, a moment for you to take a break with a local?"

Cassandra flinched at the words, but she didn't back down. "I gave you more than you gave me, Evan. Don't cry about how wounded you are now."

Evan wanted to walk away. He could still hear her anger, but it was getting drowned out by the desperation and hurt clouding his judgment. Who would have this much sway over her? How had he missed it? The only new element was Michael. What could he have done?

"What did Michael say? Give me a chance to explain it."

Cassandra started to speak and then stopped. "I'm doing what you told me to do, Evan. I'm owning the woman I am. I'm telling you that I don't want to try this anymore. You wanted me to do what is right for me, and this is it. Was that plain enough?"

"Yes," he said to her. "It's plain enough even for me."

He heard her say something, but he didn't respond. He couldn't respond. Cassandra was more than the rest of them.

She was his hope.

He needed to find out what was going on and that meant he needed some time to think.

He didn't walk back to his place in the hotel. Instead, he kept his head low and went back to his truck. When he got in his truck, he headed back home, to the outskirts, to the swampies.

Cassandra was numb. She thought about what had and hadn't happened between her and Evan, and she didn't know what to think or do.

Betrayal.

She wondered if there was something about her that made men think she was okay with it. Certainly being targeted by two completely different men meant there was something about her that said she was so desperate that she would be willing to excuse betrayal.

After dealing with the betrayal of the moment, there was the incessant need to cry. When Cassandra cried, it only validated that she was a weak person who would take betrayal. It was a vicious cycle that she experienced for about three days.

Three days later, she looked at herself in the mirror. There she saw the ravages of betrayal, pain, and some regret. She had tried to stop the regret of losing what might have been. Even though she knew it would have all been built on a lie, it was still closer to her dream than she had ever gotten.

One thing Evan was right about was that Cassandra had made some life decisions. She knew the woman she wanted to be, and she knew she wanted a man who could be honest with her. When she thought about what she needed and where she was, she knew she had done the right thing.

The problem was, she didn't feel smart. She felt alone and isolated. When she sat on her couch, memories of TV night with Evan came back to her. The bad thing about being in a one bedroom unit was that there was almost no place to go to avoid the memories. She had signed the paper and given it to Michael. Michael hadn't left yet. What his presence reminded her of was the fact that she was a CPA.

Certainly, in her emancipated mood, she should have been able to call her friends and have a goodbye toast. The problem was, every time she thought about doing a goodbye toast, she fell apart into a fit of tears. She had plenty of time to think about how she got to this point. She realized that she followed men who got her to where she was. First it was Michael, and she'd run from him. Then it was Evan. At least she didn't have to run from him. She had made the decision to leave him.

What she learned was that leaving Evan wasn't the same thing as leaving Michael. She had experienced a sense of relief when she left Michael. With Evan, she felt like she had lost her best friend. She mulled over and over why he had lied to her. It was the one thing she couldn't take, a man who couldn't be faithful. He had taken her trust and abused it.

Why did he have to be so close to the ideal?

# Thirteen

Michael took a sip of his coffee and watched as Henry ate his carrot cake. They had just finished lunch.

"I thought I was doing the right thing coming here," he said. "I was sure when I offered her all the things she had before, she would come back."

Henry used his spoon to scoop off the whipped cream that had been topped on the carrot cake. "I don't think the way to do it was by telling her the place she had settled down in was beneath her. I'm from Sweet Blooms and I like my home town."

Michael stirred his coffee. He looked around and saw a dark, dingy room. The walls were stained by old smoke and age stains. The table and chairs were wood and looked as if they had been stained by a bunch of do-it-yourselfers.

"I just wanted her to have better," Michael persisted. He couldn't understand how anyone who had known poverty would want to continue living in it. He knew what it was like to have nothing. There was nothing he would give up his standing and career for. Looking around, he started to sneer. They were all hypocrites, he thought. If someone came by and offered them a boatload of money, he knew that none of them would refuse it.

"You are about as subtle as a jackhammer," Henry said. "If this is the way you talk and persuade women, I can see why you're alone."

Michael clenched his teeth and almost snarled at Henry. "First, I'm never lacking for company. Not that it's any of your business. Second, trying to sugarcoat something has never been my way. I prefer to tell the truth the way it is. It helps everyone make informed decisions."

"Ouch! So it sounds like it's your way or the highway."

Michael stopped and looked at his coffee. "Right is right."

"I have to say, when it comes to women, sometimes…okay, most of the time, it's really not about what is logically correct. More importantly, it shouldn't be about what makes the most sense." Henry waved his spoon around as he spoke. "When I was with Hannah, I never really listened to her. She always spoke about feelings and things I thought would pass, and she would get over it. But then we had Nathan, and then all of that mushy stuff made sense, but I didn't know how to talk to Nathan that way. I tried to make money, and she kept talking about feelings. I missed some of the best moments of my son's life because I wouldn't listen.

"Now you two don't have children, but try to look at it from her point of view and see all that she's accomplished in Sweet Blooms. Give her credit for trying to find herself. I can't say I know Evan personally, but I can tell you that he has a good reputation, so that should be worth something."

"She could be so much more and make so much more money. She's not even working in the field she trained for all her life. Now she makes it seem like making money is a crime."

Henry laughed. "So since she's not embracing your values, she's sick? I think this is a place where, if you are really lucky, the two of you can be friends. Maybe you won't get her this year, but soon you will, and I think that will help you out. It helped me."

Michael thought Henry was crazy. Maybe it was something in the town that made people not think about the big picture. "Are you really going to say that being friends is an option?"

Henry finished up the last of his carrot cake. "It means that yes, I think couples can be friends. I think there comes a time when you have to ask yourself what is more important. Do you want to stay in her life or not?"

"Of course I want to stay in her life! I offered her her old life back," Michael argued.

Henry shook his head. "At this rate, you won't have her as a friend. You won't have her in your life. And let me tell you, you'll miss her."

Michael took another sip of his coffee. He thought about all the times he had met with Cassandra. She was so different than how he remembered her. He recalled how she would say it was them against the world. He thought he understood what she had been saying. He thought she understood that money was the way they could fight anything. Now he could see she had meant something else entirely.

"I think you need to give as much thought to what kind of relationship you want with Cassandra, if any at all, as you do with any business deal," Henry said, patting his stomach.

"I can do that," Michael said slowly.

"Good. Since you know business so well, you might consider this: if you wanted to get a partner to take a deal where they were going to be taking a loss, what would you do?"

Michael looked at Henry, offended. "Taking a loss?"

Henry laughed. "Well, you have to admit, having your ex hanging around while you're trying to get your life together isn't the best place for them to be."

"Who knows if he's even good enough for her?"

Henry wagged his finger and tsked at Michael. "Your business deals must go south quickly, or you must only do deals with the desperate."

Michael tapped his fingers on the table and looked at Henry. Was this what he was reduced to? Taking advice from a person like Henry, when had he accepted that he and Cassandra would never be a couple? Earlier, he hadn't been able to accept she wouldn't be a part of his life. They'd had history before all of this had happened, and Cassandra was in a category of people that was very small.

He trusted her.

"Fine, I'll try it your way," Michael said.

Clarissa lived in a small house at the end of the block. When she heard a rapping on her back door, she knew who it was. It was too late for it to be Evan, so that left only one other person.

She heard the screen door slam, and she tensed in

her kitchen. Clarissa made a habit of cleaning all the dishes in the sink before she went to bed. Her hair was in rollers, and she had on a long nightshirt that said Brains and Beauty Reside Here. Even knowing who it was didn't relax her.

"Rissa!"

Clarissa closed her eyes and tried not to get upset when she heard the name. Instead, she focused on doing the dishes.

Every dish in her house matched. If she broke a piece of the set, she'd go buy a replacement piece. The house looked like the remake of a dollhouse with the wood paneling all throughout. Her window in the kitchen was above the kitchen sink, and the kitchen itself was blue and white. On the table, there was a bowl filled with real, and fake, fruit. Even if she didn't know who it was, the rank odor of an unwashed body floated into the house ahead of him.

"What, Barrick?" she said.

She heard him stepping onto her tile floor. He must have just walked through some water or mud. When he pulled out a chair, he dragged it on her tile floor, and she had to clench her teeth not to say something.

"Why are you talking that way to me? You act like you're better. I know where you come from, Rissa!"

She didn't rise to the bait. Instead, she continued to wash the rest of the dishes. She had learned long ago there was no sense in rushing when trouble came. You couldn't stop trouble, and it was best to finish what you had started.

"Rissa, are you listening?"

"How could I not listen as loud as you are?"

"Uppity, aren't you?"

"I saw Evan. I know you're starting to hang around each other. Now, I know you're looking for a man, but I didn't think things had gotten so bad you were looking at swampies."

Clarissa felt the tears, and she blinked them away. She emptied the water in her sink and then took the dish rag, folded it over the spigot, and then took a breath before she turned around to face her half-brother, Barrick.

Barrick and Clarissa shared the same mother. Barrick's mother had fallen in love with Barrick's father. She'd thought he was so rustic. After two years in the outskirts, she'd decided that she wanted to live in town. So she'd left Barrick's father and found another husband—Clarissa's father. That wasn't enough for her either, and she left him too. Later on, Clarissa found that her mother had died of cancer and suffered from being bipolar. She regretted not being old enough to understand or help.

Clarissa thought the day she met Barrick meant they would be able to work together, but when Barrick saw Clarissa, he only saw their mother. Clarissa had been raised by a woman who said perfect was best.

Clarissa knew what the town thought about her, but it didn't matter. She would rather have them think whatever they thought than to pity her. She was left living in a house that had to be perfect. She didn't know how to do anything else but be pretty. Her father had left her with money. Fortunately, she was good at day trading. She was able to double and triple her money. She could live comfortably, but she just couldn't find anyone who wanted to be with her.

"I'm not looking to marry Evan Sparrow," she said as she took a seat.

"Then why the visits in secret?"

"If you must know, I'm helping Evan learn to read. It's always been hard and I said I would."

Barrick stopped and laughed. "You mean he doesn't know the basics, the leader of the guild? Wait until everyone finds out. I'll go to town."

"Barrick, you've got to let this jealousy go."

Barrick slammed his fist on the table.

"I guess it's easy for you to say that. You grew up in town."

Clarissa held up her hand.

"I don't want to go over the same thing again and again. I heard you. You know what it is and what's going on. Can you leave?"

Barrick picked up a banana from the basket. "Sure, I'll leave you alone for now, little sister."

When he was gone, Clarissa went to clean up the mess Barrick had made on the floor. When she was done, she went walking through the quiet house. She went to her bedroom and climbed into the four poster canopy bed. She lay there another night, wishing that for once someone would want to be with her.

Evan found it hard to focus on much except how to get Cassandra back. But he had other responsibilities that he had to take care of. One of them was to make sure the community center was renovated. While he had approached Katherine regarding money, he needed to finalize the agreement with the architect/designer. Robert had told him to contact Vihaan; he was at the Langford ranch. They were a new family coming in, but they needed their house done before they moved in.

He pulled up the drive. As he got out of the vehicle, he saw Vihaan standing on the porch kicking pillars. Evan was a little concerned when he saw the extended roof shake. Evan got out and called his name.

"Vihaan?"

The man turned around and waved to Evan. Evan could see Vihaan was toned and athletic. He was dressed in dusty blue jeans and a maroon short sleeve shirt.

"Evan?"

When Evan got to the porch, he shook Vihaan's hand.

"It's good to see you, Evan. I take it you must need something very badly to come see me here."

Evan nodded. "I'm building the community center. I need someone who will do the design work and make sure the architecture is good."

Vihaan looked at the house he was working on.

"I don't know, Evan, my schedule is pretty tight. There are three new families that are coming to Sweet Blooms. Look at this house. I don't even think we can call it that. The frame seems right, but the rest has got to go."

Evan heard him talking and watched him testing the structures that were around. Then he tapped Vihaan on the shoulder to stop him from talking. Vihaan looked up.

"If it makes a difference, Katherine is on this project."

He watched Vihaan stop, and then he thought maybe his day would start to look up.

"Does she know you're asking me?"

Evan nodded. "She knows. I told her you had accepted and the reaction was strong."

Vihaan laughed. "Evan, you have a gift for overstatement. I know Katherine. Katherine changes everything. I'll work on the project. When does it start?"

"In a couple of weeks. When I nail down some other details, I'll let you know."

Vihaan smiled. "You've got yourself a designer/architect."

Evan nodded and walked away. If only all of his problems were so easy to solve.

# Fourteen

It was time for Michael to go. He had given her the paper. She had her freedom from him and everything associated with him. He'd been angrier in the last couple of days than he'd been for a while. He had survived poor beginnings—he would survive his soon to be ex hating the sight of him.

He realized that everyone thought he was heartless. To be truthful, most of the time, he was happy making everyone believe he was. What he didn't expect was the loss he felt when it became apparent that Cassandra wasn't coming back to him. He would recover, eventually.

He would go back to what he knew. He knew numbers and money. He was sure he could find someone to appreciate those things with him. Although, after Cassandra, the thought of another woman left him hollow.

Michael thought about the people in Sweet Blooms. He couldn't live here, but he would say that they made him realize that he was missing someone he could call on. That's what Cassandra was, his friend. In this small town, they had friends.

He had associates.

He saw the bill slipped partially under the door. He opened up the door and found Henry standing there smiling at him.

"I know they say that people in small towns are slow, but I think you'd make people rethink that statement," Henry said, picking up the bill and stepping into the hotel. "So are you going back to the city so you can be bitter?"

"Henry, I'm not interested in your armchair psychology or pseudo-wisdom from the carrot cake."

Looking around the room, Henry sighed and then went to sit on the bed, leaning his back against the headboard. He didn't even take off his shoes as he propped his feet up.

"Yeah, yeah, I know. No one wants to hear what I'm saying, but I learned when you're already on the bottom, you can see things clearly. And I have to say, while I do qualify as being on the bottom, you are running a close second. So, I'll start again. You tucking tail and leaving Sweet Blooms?"

Michael gave Henry his best *you are so beneath me* stare. It had no effect. In fact, Henry picked up his hands and folded them behind his head as he waited for an answer.

"I'm not tucking tail, as you call it. I'm going home, where I belong. Cassie has made her mind up, and I've decided to respect her decision and leave." Since their last conversation, Cassie had refused to talk to him. He'd even left a message stating he had word on the papers, but she hadn't picked up or called him back. When he'd gone to the store, she had told him it wasn't a good time to talk.

Michael couldn't do anything else. He wasn't in his environment where he could surprise her with gifts or get others to help him. Cassie was making it clear he wasn't needed or wanted in her life.

"Hey, Mike?"

Michael focused on Henry on the bed. "No one has called me Mike since I was a scrawny five-year-old."

Henry smiled. "Well, maybe that's the problem, because I have to tell you, you are acting like a scrawny five-year-old in a grown man's body. You won't get her back as your wife, but don't lose a friendship that you really need."

"Cassie has changed, and she doesn't want to be around me. I remind her of everything she left."

"Ouch! Do you?"

"Do I what?"

"Do you remind her of all she left?"

Michael was about to say he was all that was good, but then he gave it some thought and remembered that Cassie had told him he made her feel small.

"Thinking on it, she could be right," he admitted. "I'd like to add that I'm determined, and goal orientated, and my career is very important to me."

Henry laughed. "The funny thing is, you two are a lot alike. She's determined, a hard worker, and likes to finish things."

"Then she should come home and make money doing it!"

"The issue is, she is home. And money isn't all that important. Have you seen her in the store in the last day or so?"

Michael nodded his head. "Yes, and she didn't want to see me."

"Did she say that?"

"No, but—"

"Did you notice if she was happy or sad?"

Michael stopped. "Sad? Cassie has no reason –"

Henry held up his hand. "I didn't ask you what you thought. I asked you if you had stopped thinking about yourself long enough to see Cassandra."

Michael went over to the chair in the room and took a seat. Was Cassie sad? He recalled seeing her in the store. It was true she hadn't been smiling, but he just attributed that to living in the town. What if it wasn't that? Her voice had been monotone, and she hadn't been as peppy. Michael looked at Henry sitting on the bed, looking up at the ceiling.

Then Henry faced Michael. Michael pointed to himself. "Oh, do you want me to say something? You obviously want to say something, so go ahead."

"Cassandra and Evan broke up."

Michael leaned forward. "What?"

Henry shook his head. "I'm not telling you so you can try and get her back. I'm telling you because she may need a friend."

Michael sat back and thought on the idea that he had been so wrapped up in himself that he hadn't noticed that Cassie was unhappy. Michael looked up at a smiling Henry who was wiggling his eyebrows.

"You're right. Before I leave, I'll check in on her. I'll give her the option, if she wants to hang out with an old friend."

Henry clapped his hands. "Great! I'm glad we both came to the conclusion that I'm right. Let's go eat, and you can pay."

Michael looked at the happy Henry who had sprung up from the bed. Henry had his hand on the front door, but then he looked behind him.

"You need to get something?" Henry asked Michael.

Michael looked at Henry and shook his head. Henry's smile got wider, and he opened the door as he began to talk.

"First, when we go downstairs, I think you should cover the bill for one more night. Second, I heard about this place that is a bit far, but I hear the food is good. It's too rich for my blood, but since you're paying –"

Cassandra was thinking about getting a new place. Coming home after work was a dread. She found herself trying to work later so she would come home exhausted. It never worked, but she tried anyway. Cassandra would have given anything a try to come home and fall blissfully asleep. Instead, her nights were torturous walks down memory lane.

Just when she thought she was over it, a smell would trigger it all back. Or one of the many carvings she had now would pull him back into her thoughts. Tonight she was going to try something new. She hadn't seen Evan in a couple of days, and it was time to break physically what had already been emotionally severed.

She went into her bedroom and got the bracelet that Evan had made her. She held it in her hands and remembered what was. They had been through so many ups and downs, and she thought for sure this was the right choice to make. Heaving a deep sigh, she reached for the bracelet to pull it apart. When the beads fell all over the place, she'd bury it in the yard to give herself some sort of closure. She picked the bracelet up and her intercom rang.

It was probably Michael. He had been by a couple of times, but she hadn't even been able to concentrate on what he was saying. Her days were just a blur now that she was away from Evan. Shaking her head, she looked at the bracelet and then pulled when the intercom rang again. She put the bracelet down and went to the intercom.

"Cassandra, it's me."

She yanked her hand back from the intercom as if it were a snake. Why would Evan come here? Why tonight?

She stood next to the buzzer until it rang again. When she clicked the button, she heard him.

"I can stay here all night if that's what it takes."

She thought about him being out there, and she relented.

"What do you want?"

"I want to have a conversation face to face."

"Why?"

"Cassandra, please." If he had been belligerent, angry, or in some way a jerk, she could have told him no in a heartbeat, but this…

"Come up."

As she heard him taking the steps, she knew what she was going to do. She was going to politely listen to him and then tell him to leave. She had already explained it all, but this would be the final straw.

She had unlocked the door and was sitting on the couch. All the thoughts she had on how she was going to deal with him went out the window as soon as she saw him open her front door.

Seeing him caused that restless thing in her soul to quiet down and the woman who had been missing him to perk up. He was the man who made her smile. The man she could laugh with. The man she thought looked amazing all the time. Right now he looked like a man on a mission.

He came in and closed the door behind him.

"We are going to have an open and honest conversation."

She blinked. "Now? You want to have one of these conversations now?"

"Yes, I'd like one right now. If the best thing that ever happened to me is going to go away, I want to be clear on why."

After he said those words, Cassandra felt like she separated into two. One part of her felt like she wanted to throw him out, but the other part of her was jumping for joy that he knew she was the best thing that would ever happen to him.

"We just don't —"

He held up his hand to stop her. He walked over and sat on the couch. When he sat down, the bracelet rolled towards him. He picked it up and rolled the beads between his fingertips.

"I made this bracelet for you. Each one of these beads is a picture about you."

Cassandra leaned closer to see the pictures on the beads.

"Every figure you see on each bead represents something about you. The flower is your beauty, the lion is your strength, the bird is your free spirit. Nothing about this bracelet was an accident. I knew it was for you and only you. I want you to know I still believe those things even now."

Cassandra looked at the beads and thought about what Michael had said. Well, she must not be as special as he claimed because Clarissa had a bracelet too. She couldn't stop the tears from clouding her view. She closed her eyes to try and stop the tears from falling, but it did no good. When the first tear dropped, Evan caught it.

"Don't cry, Cassandra. I don't know what it is that I'm saying, but don't cry. You have to know that all I want to do is make you as happy as you've made me."

Cassandra looked up through the haze of tears.

"If that's true, why did you give Clarissa a bracelet? Why the secret of you and Clarissa?"

"Who told you about the bracelet?"

"It doesn't matter who told me. It matters that I've got an engagement bracelet, and so does she and –"

"She doesn't."

"Are you saying that she doesn't have a bracelet?"

"No, she does."

"Did you give her that bracelet in the last year?"

"Yes, I did."

Cassandra pulled back. "Then we have nothing to –"

"Wait. Listen to me."

Cassandra looked at him. What could he say? Her heart was shattering into smaller and smaller pieces. "What could you say?" she heard herself ask, but the sound was more like a wounded animal than anything else.

"The bracelet was just a thank you."

Cassandra drew back from him. "You give a beautiful woman like Clarissa an engagement bracelet as a thank you. Well, whatever she did, I'm glad she didn't go overboard because you might have given her a wedding ring to make sure she knew how much you appreciated her."

Evan looked upward and then at her. "Cassandra, have you even seen her bracelet?"

"No, I haven't."

"It's got white beads with a simple design."

"How does that make it any better? This bracelet was supposed to be special and —"

"It is."

"But Clarissa has one."

Evan ran his hands through his hair. "Cassandra, I can't read," he murmured.

Cassandra thought she'd heard him correctly, but she was having a hard time believing it.

"What are you talking about?"

"I'm saying that I can't read. Clarissa reads contracts for me and makes sure they are correct."

Cassandra heard him but just couldn't seem to reconcile what he was saying with the man before her.

"It can't be. You drive—"

"Do you remember the first time you told me to go down a street? I missed the street. I missed it because I can't read the signs. I can get anywhere in town because I know every place. When you came to town, I decided to try to learn. I can read basic words slowly, but not a lot. I wanted to say thank you to Clarissa for helping me, so I made her a bracelet that looks like a kids' bracelet as a gift."

There were no words to describe how she felt. She was delirious that he wasn't in a relationship with Clarissa, but she was also in disbelief over what he was saying. Evan was the most put together person she knew. How could she have not known?

"Why didn't you ask me?"

Evan laughed mirthlessly. "I couldn't ask you to help

me read. I wanted to show you I could take care of you and any kids we had. I don't think that confidence comes when a man says, 'I want to be with you forever and, by the way, can you spell that or read it because I can't.'"

"Evan," she said compassionately.

"And I didn't want that tone either. It's in between wonder and pity."

"Evan, I could never pity you."

"I care about you, Cassandra. I don't want to lose our opportunity."

"You're right. It makes a difference, but maybe we are too different. Maybe we have a difference in what we expect from life."

"That doesn't sound like you, Cassandra. I told you mine. It's your turn to tell me yours," he said.

"What if there is nothing to tell?" she asked.

"You sound like your husband."

"He's not my husband," she said through clenched teeth in response.

"Well, it sounds like all of the things he would say are the words that happen to be coming out of your mouth now. I'm not asking you to go on faith. I'm asking you to look at what we've been doing together. We are here because we want to be with each other. We see something in each other that makes this all worth it."

She swallowed. "I'm scared. How did you know that I'd been talking to Michael?"

"Because you were talking about going backward in time. I've never known you to be scared of anything. But ever since Michael has come to town, you've been second guessing yourself. If we've moved every other obstacle and you're still not sure, this tells me you've let him get in your head. He doesn't think I'm good enough for you. And I have to say that I agree with him."

Cassandra laughed through her tears. "You're both wrong. Evan, you're not just good for me, you're what I need."

Evan patted her hand and placed the bracelet back in her palm.

"You should know that not everyone knows that I can't read well. They assume because I'm from the outskirts that I just read slow."

"Do you want to learn how to read and write fluently?"

Evan smiled and nodded his head.

Cassandra smiled also. "We'll work on it together, and by the time someone figures it out, we'll be done and past that."

His hand still covered hers. Cassandra could feel the bracelet in her hand, and it was the focal point of it all. She knew now what the bracelet meant. If she took it now, she would be saying they were back together again. She would be saying that she forgave him for not telling her the whole truth about Clarissa. She looked into his eyes and saw him waiting.

Pushing aside all doubts, she curled her hand around the bracelet. She heard the sigh of relief from Evan and then she was pulled into his arms. A light kiss was placed on the back of her neck and she let herself fall into the comfort of his arms.

When he pulled back to look into her eyes, she knew he could see the tears shimmering in her eyes. When she saw him bending down to give her a kiss, she didn't move back. Instead, she waited to feel his mouth on hers. When their lips finally touched, her hands traced his wrists and went up to his arms. As his lips brushed against hers, a need to reaffirm the commitment they had just made to each other turned into a promise. As he deepened the kiss, she found her hands clinging to his shoulders. When he drew back and stared into her eyes, he spoke.

"Tell me this means what I think it means."

Cassandra smiled at him and nodded. "It means another stimulating night of Mulan, absolutely!"

He laughed and pulled her into his embrace. When she had come home that night, if you had asked her if this outcome was possible, she would have said no. Now Cassandra clung tighter as she held on to her future.

# Fifteen

Evan had a new view on life after last night. He realized that fear of what others thought had almost made him lose Cassandra. Evan had hoped that Michael had already left town. As he stood in front of Michael's door, it proved his hopes wouldn't be realized today.

When Michael opened the door, he saw Evan and stepped aside for them to talk. Now Evan was looking at the man who had been Cassandra's husband. According to Cassandra, this was the man who, no matter what else he had done, had been the one to help her through school. He had been the one to convince her to follow the path of accounting, even though her family had wanted her to do business. For all of his faults, Evan had to realize that if it hadn't been for this man, Cassandra wouldn't be in Sweet Blooms.

Evan had taken the time to look up Michael as well. He was respected and even feared in some arenas. He had a reputation of being a miracle worker—if you could afford it. When it came to pure grit, considering how far he'd had to come, Michael had Evan's respect. Evan felt as though it was even. Michael was determined to make money like he was determined to get and keep Cassandra.

Michael took a seat at the small table and waited.

Evan took a seat at the table and looked at Michael, his hands open.

"I want to say I understand why you came back for Cassandra. Anyone who knows Cassandra understands that. I don't expect us to be best friends, but I would like for us to be cordial if for no other reason than Cassandra," he said.

Evan waited for Michael to say something. He didn't know how this would end, but he knew that if Michael sent him out of the room right now, he would leave knowing he had tried to make peace with an important part of Cassandra's past.

Michael tapped his fingers on the table and then let out a sigh.

"I could have chosen a different way to come to town." Michael straightened his neck and cleared his throat. "I had a vision that Cassandra would do what she had always done: come back to me. I didn't look at how everyone treated her. I only thought about how she was with me and what I needed."

Michael held his hands out and drew in a shaky breath. "I never thought beyond that…" Looking at Evan, he shook his head. "It's funny how self-absorbed you can become." He cleared his throat and looked around the room. "You don't know me, but I didn't grow up like Cassandra. I thought when she met me and saw where I came from, she'd understand. Instead, she did something that was totally Cassandra. She didn't even notice where I came from. She only noticed me."

Evan nodded as he thought about Cassandra. She'd been through a lot, but Cassandra was still herself. That inner goodness and giving spirit couldn't be crushed.

"I didn't do right by her," Michael said quietly. "She was there for me no matter what. I was wrong, and I should have been there for her, for the things that mattered to her, not just the things that mattered to me. I should have done better by her."

Evan heard the words and nodded. It didn't make what he had done to Cassandra right, but it gave him something so he could understand.

"I plan on doing right by her."

"So you want to be friends?" Michael asked. "I mean, this seems more like a Cassandra move than yours, but I'm open to it," he said with a smile.

Evan had a moment where he thought about saying no and telling Michael to have a good trip, but in the end, what mattered was Cassandra. Evan knew there was still more to do. More to say to Michael. He could come up with a ton of reasons to walk away, but all of them paled next to looking into Cassandra's eyes to tell her he'd done his best to make this right.

"I'm not good enough for Cassandra. Neither one of us is," Evan said. "I want you to know I'm a functional illiterate. It means I have a problem reading –"

"I know what it means."

"Now you know, and there are no more secrets. I'm not good enough, but I'm working on it. If and when you and Cassandra come to terms, I want you to know I'll support that," Evan said.

"I'm not really sure I buy into that."

"You don't have to. If you want to know why I'm doing it, the answer is Cassandra."

Michael folded his hands in his lap. "I'm leaving, but I'll try to see Cassie."

Evan tried to stop the groan hearing that name

caused. "You might try saying her name as Cassandra because she really doesn't like Cassie."

"Well, I'll work on it," Michael replied with a smile. Evan wasn't sure what would come of this, but he was sure that he had done all there was to do. The rest was just time. Evan stood up and held out his hand to Michael.

Michael grabbed it, and they both shook.

Michael gave Evan a second look. "You should know, I don't think I would have done what you've done today. Come and try to make friends, yes. But come over and tell you that I had a weakness, no. I think it took a lot of guts to do that."

Evan nodded and walked out of the room. It was like a weight off of his shoulders to have told Cassandra and now to have tried laying the groundwork to mend the fence with Michael. All he wanted to do was see Cassandra, and they were scheduled for lunch. He couldn't wait.

He'd just finished doing some drawings at the center. All day he'd meant to find Ms. Waters to go over the terms and the placement of the classrooms, but they kept missing each other. When he walked into the store to see Cassandra and go to lunch, much to his dismay, there was Ms. Waters.

"Oh, Mr. Sparrow, I'm so glad you showed up," Ms. Waters said. Evan knew something was wrong. She was calling him by his last name, and she had a glint in her eye that didn't make him feel any better.

"Evan, Ms. Waters said she has been talking to Barrick and going over some terms that she thought might be better than what you all had originally agreed on," Cassandra said. Evan could see she was a bit worried. When he looked at Ms. Waters, he could see she had some papers in her hand and knew that didn't bode well for him. He was okay with telling Cassandra and Michael about his issue, but if his issue was mentioned here in the store, the whole town would know. Evan wasn't ready for that yet.

"I'm sure we can look at whatever new things you want. If you leave the paperwork with me, I'll go over it and then get back to you," Evan said.

Ms. Waters pasted on a saccharine smile that Evan could see had a hint of maliciousness in it. "No, I think it's important we fix this now. Barrick told me that the longer I wait, the harder it would be for the guild to do any changes."

It was then that Evan knew she knew about his problem. He didn't know what she hoped to gain from it, but he wasn't going to run. It wasn't the way he would have wanted this to happen. Looking at Cassandra, he could see her preparing, and she nodded her head slightly and smiled.

"Ms. Waters, the truth is —"

The bell went off in the store. Evan didn't turn around to see who it was. Then he felt a hand on his shoulder.

"The truth is, giving an immediate decision on financials is never a good idea, and it's not something that Evan can do," Michael said.

Evan turned to see Michael standing there with a smile on his face. He even had the gall to wink at him.

This afternoon was just getting better and better, Evan thought sarcastically. Evan looked at Cassandra, and he could see she was trying to hide a smile.

Ms. Waters looked at Michael, and Evan could see she was attracted to him and upset that he had interrupted. Her eyes had lingered a little too long on Michael.

"I don't know who you are, sir, but I don't think this matter is of any concern to you." After summarily dismissing Michael, she turned back to Evan.

"Mr. Sparrow," Waters said. "I think you should review the information here. If you can," she added, her voice rising with each word until everyone in the store had stopped and was directly or indirectly looking at them.

Again, Michael interjected by stepping in front of Evan. Holding out his hand, he spoke to Ms. Waters.

"Forgive me for being so rude. I didn't catch your name," Michael said. At first, Evan thought she wouldn't answer, but then she put her hand in his. Michael pulled it to his nose.

"Ah, I don't know your name, but I know you have very good taste. A fragrance says a lot about a woman. It's Chanel No. 5, no?"

Evan backed away and made his way to stand next to Cassandra behind the counter. When he got there, she grabbed his hand. Evan leaned over to Cassandra's ear and whispered, "He's good."

Cassandra looked at him and smiled. "He's not even trying." The both of them looked back at Sandra and Michael.

"My name is Ms. Sandra Waters. I am the owner of the community center. Evan and his kind will make the necessary items we need to keep the center open. They owe it to me since they built the wood shop on the Cade place."

Michael nodded after releasing her hand. "I can see

your point and how this must all seem so very unfair to you. However, asking Evan to look at projections from…who did you say?"

"Barrick. He's one of them, you know, outskirters."

"Yes, I can see it all clearly now," Michael said. "I'm not sure you want Evan to look at numbers from this individual. Are you sure the numbers are in your favor? I mean, I can look at the numbers."

Ms. Waters perked up and shook her head. "No, I want him to do it here in the store for everyone to see. I think he's being manipulated by Robert anyway."

Michael nodded. "I can see your point. Well, I have to tell you that one of the many things I'm here to do in town is act on Evan's behalf when it comes to figures and numbers. So you see, Evan wouldn't be able to look at those numbers without getting in legal trouble and breaking my contract."

Evan leaned over Cassandra and whispered again. "I believe it."

Cassandra elbowed him in the side.

Sandra Waters looked at Michael, and she shook her head. For a moment she looked at Evan and Cassandra, and in that moment, Evan saw her accept the knowledge that she had lost her objective.

Turning back to Michael, she finished the conversation. "Thank you, kind sir, for looking out for me. It's rare in this day. I'll wait until a better time to review the numbers." With that, Ms. Waters left the store. There was almost a sigh of regret from the customers. Then Skye came out from the back.

"Okay everyone, for your patience, if you have an item in your hand, bring it up and you'll get ten percent off."

The counter was flooded by a line, and Skye smiled at the three of them.

Michael spoke first. "That woman is good."

Cassandra looked at him with a raised eyebrow. "Don't get any ideas. She's already taken by an amazing man."

Michael put his hand to his chest.

"Oh, is that to insinuate I'm not amazing?"

Cassandra laughed. "I wouldn't tell you anything else to make your head any bigger than it naturally is."

The both of them laughed, and Evan looked at them both. A couple of days ago, had anyone asked him if Cassandra, her ex, and he would be laughing together, they would have taken bets on how unlikely that would be. Looking at Cassandra's smile, he realized that once love is in your life, all things were possible.

# Sixteen

The next morning, Cassandra, Evan, and Michael went over the numbers from Ms. Waters. Then Cassandra went to work. So much had happened so quickly. She couldn't believe it. Evan had done everything he said he would, and now Cassandra felt it was her turn. She had been touching her bracelet all day. She asked Evan to meet her after work.

It was six o'clock, and her get up and go had got up and gone. The day had been filled with difficult customers. Skye had needed to leave her alone for a couple of hours in the shop as she and Caleb figured out what to do about wedding plans.

The day was filled with people who asked the same questions about the same products. Between running to the cash register and then being on the floor, she had been moving constantly. By the time the end of the day rolled around, she almost forgot she had told Evan to meet her. It was his text asking if he could meet her in front of the store that reminded her she needed to see him and clear the air.

She had finally finished packing up the last order, and Skye gave her the nod so she could leave for the day.

As she put on her sweater, she started to get her second wind. When she opened the door, Evan was there waiting for her with a smile.

"Rough day?" he asked.

"I look that bad?"

"You never look bad, but you do have some days where that smile isn't as big," he joked. He walked them up the street so they could find some seating. When they were seated, he moved his chair closer to her and leaned over to kiss her on the cheek.

"Cassandra, talk to me."

She held her hand out on the table and tapped the bracelet. He looked at it, confused.

"We need to talk about this," she said. He looked at her and then ran his hands over the beads on her wrist.

He looked at her and smiled. "I have to tell you, starting with that phrase was not the way to put me at ease."

"Don't stress. If I'm doing this right, we should both feel better."

"I'm listening."

"These last couple of days have been amazing. I feel like we have gotten so much closer and I couldn't be happier," Cassandra said.

When she saw Evan let out a breath, Cassandra almost laughed out loud but she didn't want him to interrupt what she wanted to say. Evan deserved this moment.

"I want to give you back your bracelet." She took it off and placed it in his hand.

"I hope this is ending up the way I think it is."

"We won't know if you don't let me finish," she said, laughing.

"Okay, go ahead."

"I don't need the year and a day to know you are the one for me. Evan Sparrow, will you marry me?"

"You weren't on one knee, but yes! You know I have to make you another piece now that we're going to be married."

She shook her head. "I think we can marry first and give the gift later."

He looked at her as if she had just spoken in another language. "Now hold up. I am beyond happy that you're ready to marry but we can't throw away tradition."

Cassandra looked at him a second time. "Tell me you're kidding."

He smiled at her. "Yeah, I am."

She threw herself into his arms. "Don't play like that."

When she let him go, he looked at her and caressed her face. "Just when I think you can't make me happier, you do. Thank you. In case you didn't know, and you needed me to say it, Cassandra Olsen, I love you."

"You invited me to the hotel bar?" Cassandra asked Michael.

"It's my last day, and I wanted to have one last talk with you."

Cassandra couldn't say she'd ever been in this part of the hotel. The walls were a dark beige, but she had a feeling they hadn't started out that way. Time had left its smudges on the walls. Although normally she wouldn't consider ordering from a place where she couldn't see, this was a time she was thinking it might be a better idea if she didn't see anything.

"Well, thanks for inviting me," Cassandra said. "It's a new experience."

"You were always polite," Michael said.

Just then, Henry walked over to the table. "Lookie here. I didn't think you knew anyone who would be seen with you in public," Henry said.

Cassandra laughed. "I like you already."

Henry laughed.

Michael interrupted. "Henry, this is my friend. Cassandra –"

Cassandra looked at Michael and smiled. "I actually already know Henry. I've seen him around with Hannah and Nathan. But it is nice to meet you again."

"Same here," Henry said.

Henry turned to Michael. "Didn't know you had any friends in Sweet Blooms. So nice to know that old dogs can learn new tricks," Henry said, nodding to Michael.

"I'll have you know that in other places, my company is sought after and there are many people who will say they are my friend, in public," Michael protested.

"I'll leave you two to your conversation. I hope you have a great day," Henry said as he walked away.

Cassandra felt him looking at her, and she waited for him to speak. "Well, we don't have to order. I'm not sure I feel okay risking your health."

"You're leaving?"

"Yes, I am."

Cassandra reached out to him. "Thank you, Michael. I want to tell you something."

Michael sighed. "You've got that sweet tone that says you're trying to ease into a topic you think I won't like."

Cassandra smarted on how well he knew her. "What I'm going to tell you is that as soon as we have everything straightened out, I'm going to marry Evan."

Michael smiled at her. "I think you two are great together. I respect him as a man, and I think he's good for you, just like this town."

Cassandra stopped and looked at Michael again as if she were waiting for him to morph into another person. "You're okay with it?"

"Yes, I finally am okay with it. I can see that all this is good for you."

"Great."

"Good. I hope that the two of you can make it work."

"I'll see you around, Michael."

"Yes, I'll see you around, Cass… Cassandra."

Cassandra got up and left the hotel. The sun was shining, and the world was all of a sudden a better place.

Epilogue

Vihaan helped his father, Jerry, pull the benches from the storage shed to the backyard. They had brought out several of the tables and benches. His family was here, and it was time to eat. Vihaan was an only child, but his mother, Geeta, came from a large family. He had seven aunts and three uncles.

All of them had children, which meant he never lacked for cousins. When they came over, it was amazing, but when they left, Vihaan was very aware of how different and alone he was in the town of Sweet Blooms.

After his father had stood up and put his hands on his aching back, his cousin Suhana came out with table cloths.

"Uncle Jerry, go in. I'll finish up and help Vihaan out here."

Vihaan's father nodded and went in. Vihaan looked at Suhana and smiled.

"Nice move," he said. "Just in time for me to help you put out all of the tablecloths. But I think you wanted something else."

"Because you don't answer your phone and can't find

time to go to lunch, I am reduced to these tactics," she said with a smile. Vihaan couldn't imagine Suhana being reduced. She had mocha skin, a smile that never faltered, and she wore her dark hair up in a bun that made everyone wonder how long her hair was. She was a breath of sunshine wherever she went.

"What is it, Suhana?"

"Tell me what keeps you so busy that you can't call family."

Vihaan looked at Suhana and sighed. Out of all of the cousins, they were the closest.

"The woman of my dreams."

Suhana smiled. "I suspected as much. How long have you two been dating?"

Vihaan shook his head. "I'm afraid my journey won't be that easy, Suhana. If I had to describe her intentions towards me, I'd be very careful about any deep holes."

Suhana covered her mouth to hide the shock. "What have you done?"

Vihaan smiled. "I think the thing that she is holding against me is that I told her she was smart."

Suhana looked at him with an odd smile.

"Why didn't you compliment her on her beauty?"

Vihaan stopped stretching out the tablecloth and shrugged.

"I didn't compliment her on her beauty because everyone can see that. But I see her, and the most amazing things about her can't be seen on the outside."

Suhana laughed. "Oh yes, cousin. You are truly hooked."

I hope you've enjoyed Evan and Cassandra's story. Check out Book six in the Love Happens Series *Sweet Favors* and read about Vihaan and Katherine's story.

Sign up to my newsletter to receive updates on new releases, sale promotions, and free books.

susanwarnerauthor.com

www.ingramcontent.com/pod-product-compliance
Lightning Source LLC
Chambersburg PA
CBHW060801210726
48292CB00013B/1619